The Pursuit

by
Samantha Powers

The Capitol Love Series
Book 2

Copyright © 2016 Samantha Powers
Cover art copyright © 2016 Tim Ford

ISBN: 978-0986182259

Published and distributed
by Possibilities Publishing Company

www.possibilitiespublishingcompany.com

This is a work of fiction.

For Jeannie, who never shied away from adventure.

Chapter 1

It was a sticky, sweaty August morning in Washington, D.C., and as Rayne Michael got ready for work, she felt the city's lethargy seeping in. Everything seemed to be moving slowly, if it was moving at all. Nothing much happened in the doldrums of late August, and she had no reason to think today would be any different. If anything was looming on her horizon, she hoped it was a thunderstorm that would break through this heat.

She took a cool shower then put on a vintage flowered sundress, sandals, and sunglasses and headed out the door carrying a plastic to-go cup full of iced tea with lots of lemon and sugar. Despite the heat, there was a soft breeze so she decided to walk from her house in the Eastern Market neighborhood to her office near Stanton Park. It was less than a mile, and she could use the exercise. Besides, this time of year, the subway was a mad crush of tourists and cranky office workers, and she always seemed to end up in the one car whose air conditioning was on the fritz. She'd much rather breathe fresh air even if it was a bit swampy.

As she reached the corner, an elderly woman waved to her from the front porch of her house.

"Good morning, Ms. Rayne," the woman called. Then she pointed with her cane at the streetlight. "It's working!"

"Oh, that's wonderful, Miss Ada!" Rayne stopped at the iron gate in front of the woman's house and looked up to admire the now-functioning streetlight. She had called various city departments to complain and finally contacted the local city council member a week ago, arguing that having a broken streetlight made Ada feel less safe in her own home and affected the whole block. Now she could see that not only had the bulb and glass globe been replaced but the city had put a metal cage over it to keep mischievous kids—or worse—from breaking it again.

Ada walked down the porch steps leaning heavily on her cane and came to meet Rayne at the gate.

"I was hoping I'd catch you this morning," Ada said. "I made blueberry muffins." She handed Rayne a bundle wrapped up in a paper towel. "I know you youngsters don't always take time for a proper breakfast."

"You are too sweet!" Rayne said. "And you're right, I forgot all about breakfast."

The woman smiled at her, then held a tissue to her mouth as she coughed for a long minute. Rayne studied her face with concern.

"Are you feeling any better?" she asked.

"It's this heat," Ada said in a choked voice. "I'll be fine once it cools off."

"That could be weeks from now!" Rayne said. "Maybe you should have your son take you to the doctor."

Ada waved a hand in gentle dismissal of Rayne's suggestion. "He's got better things to do. Now you have yourself a nice day at work, Ms. Rayne."

Rayne leaned over the gate and kissed the woman on the cheek. "I will, and you be sure to let me know if you need anything else."

She continued on her way at a slow, steady pace, careful not to break into a sweat. She passed the Library of Congress and the Supreme Court, where tourists were already lining up to get inside. The sun was hot on her arms, and she longed for cooler weather. Late summer in D.C. always seemed to have her craving a change of scenery, though fortunately she could easily satisfy it with a trek to the National Mall or Rock Creek Park.

When she was growing up, she and her parents had moved often, experimenting with communes and a series of loosely knit collections of like-minded people who wanted to live off the grid—even if that meant living in a school bus—and grow their own food and leave the rest of the world behind. She had happy memories of many of the places, but she wished they'd stayed someplace—anyplace—long enough for her to put down roots, maybe worm her way into a clique, or even run for secretary of her class.

Now she was happy to have settled in D.C., and she loved her job as media relations manager at the Center for Action on Climate Change. Life was good and predictable, and that was just the way she wanted it.

When she got near Union Station, she veered east, away from the tourist zone and into the Stanton Park neighborhood. A couple blocks later, she turned off the sidewalk onto the brick pathway that led to her office. It was in a historic house that had been built in the 1800s for a merchant who made a small fortune in the import/export business. But she preferred to think of him as a sea captain and often pictured him like Ahab, wooden leg and all, standing at the upstairs bay window, gazing toward the Chesapeake Bay and the ocean beyond, and longing to be back at sea.

In truth, he was more likely surveying the city or maybe the port of Alexandria to the southwest and tallying up receipts in his head.

She stepped inside and glanced into the small parlor/office on the left to say hello to Sheila, CACC's executive assistant, but she wasn't at her desk. Jeremy, the president, worked in a study behind the parlor, but that door was closed. Rayne was about to head up the stairs to her office when Sheila burst out of Jeremy's office. Rayne immediately knew something was amiss. Despite only being in her mid-thirties, Sheila had the sort of graceful efficiency of a bygone era of secretarial pools and cashmere twinsets. Jeremy couldn't function without her. But now Sheila was racing across the room toward Rayne, who couldn't remember her ever moving that fast.

"Jeremy needs to see you," Sheila said. "Right away."

"What's up?" Rayne asked, feeling alarmed.

"It's better if he explains it." Sheila took her by the hand and led her into Jeremy's office.

He was standing with his back to the door, staring out the ceiling-to-floor window. His dark hair looked like he'd raked his hands through it one time too many, but under any condition, he was one of the handsomest men Rayne had ever known. She'd had a crush on him since the moment she'd stepped into that office two years ago to interview for the job, but she was content to keep it to herself. It was one of those things that made her look forward to going to work but not something she ever felt the need to act on.

He turned away from the window and smiled at her, but it was a regretful sort of smile. At least, that's what Rayne thought. She looked at Sheila questioningly, but Sheila shook her head, walked out, and closed the door behind her.

"Is something wrong?" Rayne asked.

Jeremy sat down at his desk—an old, majestic thing made of oak that had belonged to the sea captain himself. Rayne sat down in the leather armchair across from him and set her iced tea on the carpeted floor rather than risk marring the desk.

"Remember how I told you that our ten-year lease is up next month," Jeremy said, "and I was afraid Vincent might raise the rent on us?"

"Yes," Rayne said. The landlord had given them a deal that was well below the market rate. He claimed at the time that he genuinely cared about climate change, but they all suspected it was really because he wanted the tax write-off.

"Well, he didn't raise the rent," Jeremy said.

"That's good—"

"He cancelled the lease altogether."

"What? Why?"

Jeremy placed his hands on the edge of the desk. "He says he wants to carve the house up into condos because, to use his words, 'These hipster millennials will pay anything to say they live in a converted historic building.'"

Rayne felt as though the wind had been knocked right out of her. The thought that this charming house, which had stood for well over a hundred years, could be converted into more overpriced condos was heartbreaking.

"Even if we could find a comparable property in the District," Jeremy said, "we can't afford to pay full rent." He studied her for a moment, and the look on his face made her feel a sudden queasy flush of heat.

"The truth is," Jeremy said, "we're barely staying afloat as it is."

The organization had never been extravagant, and all the employees tended to be judicious about office supplies and expense reports, but she'd always thought it was part of the conservation ethic.

"What do you mean?" she asked.

He looked away from her. "I mean we'll have to fold."

She was stunned. "Fold? It can't be as bad as all that."

He stood and walked over to the window again, and Rayne couldn't shake the image of the old sea captain.

"In the ten years since I started this organization," he said, "we've built up some street cred and a group of very devoted donors, and that's been enough to keep us going but only if we don't have any unexpected expenses. And full rent in the District is a doozy of an unexpected expense."

"Couldn't we find another place like this one, with a landlord who's willing to give us a break?" she asked, but as soon as she said it, she realized how unlikely it was given the hot real estate market in the District.

Jeremy shook his head. "I'm going to sit down with Larry," he said, referring to their CFO, "and go over our finances and options, but I'm trying to be realistic. And I wanted you to know right away in case anyone in the media gets wind of this and comes calling."

Rayne was silent for a moment. "And what do you want me to say if they do?"

"Tell them that we are looking into various options but that our hope is the landlord will reconsider and at the very least, keep this local treasure intact," Jeremy said. "Put your spin on it, of course. Oh, and keep this to yourself for the time being. I don't want to alert the whole staff until I have more information."

"Of course," she said and stood up to go. She grabbed her bag and iced tea from the floor and glanced over to see him watching her thoughtfully.

He smiled. "I had more experienced applicants when I hired you, but there was something in your eyes. I knew you felt the same passion I did about the mission. I knew you would fight the good fight with me. And you have."

Rayne felt tears beginning to build behind her eyes. This sounded like goodbye. "I'm not done fighting yet," she said.

She walked slowly up the stairs to her office, which was in a former bedroom. Later owners had added a bathroom fifty years ago, and she kept it stocked with handmade soaps and pretty towels so that many of the other employees preferred to traipse through her office rather than use the more utilitarian bathroom on the first floor. She didn't mind because it meant she got to talk to just about all her co-workers in the course of the day.

But now she did something she rarely ever did: She shut her office door. She didn't want to have to lie if anyone came by and asked why she looked so glum.

She set her iced tea on the desk and turned on her computer. It was a little old and a little slow, so while it booted up, she nibbled on Ada's blueberry muffin as she went over her to-do list for the day, but she was having a hard time focusing. When her computer was finally ready to go, she opened a new document and monkeyed with the wording of the response she would give any reporter who called for a comment on the organization's situation. But nothing she wrote made sense. So she tinkered with a press release about a new research report one of the organization's analysts had just written, called the council member's office to thank her for Ada's streetlight, and spent some time updating the contact info for her media list just because it was mindless work.

But all the while she felt her neat, settled little world slipping away.

Lunch time came and went, but she didn't have the energy or the appetite to go out and get anything. In mid-afternoon, she went downstairs to the kitchen for some water and saw Larry leaving Jeremy's office with a stack of folders and a grim expression.

Later, she caught herself sitting at her desk just staring into space. It was only 4:00, but she was thinking about leaving a little early when her cell phone beeped. She pulled it out to see a message from her best friend and housemate Savannah, which brought the first smile to her face in hours.

Happy hour @Zipped?? Savannah asked.

Rayne immediately typed back, *Yes! That's just what I need. What time?*

I'm already here, Savannah texted back, followed by a blushing smiley emoji.

On my way!

Rayne tucked her phone away, powered down her computer, and grabbed her bag. As she headed down the stairs, she wondered what drink Savannah's boyfriend Colin would fix for her. He was the bartender—and owner—of Zipped and the wine bar Balance&Bite, and he had an uncanny gift for knowing the perfect drink a person needed in any situation.

Whatever he chose, she hoped he'd make it a double. And she felt a glimmer of excitement at the thought that his sexy brother Chase might also be there. Tall, muscular Chase with the soulful blue eyes, shaggy brown hair, and a smile that melted hearts all over town. He had a reputation for being a player, but that did little to dampen her spirits. She needed something fun to look forward to.

Chapter 2

Chase stuffed his laptop into a shoulder bag and left the apartment. He could have easily done what he needed to do at home, but he was craving a change of scenery so he started walking to Sweet Happens Café.

He'd been in D.C. for most of the summer with only a couple short jaunts on photography assignments out West, and he was starting to get restless. For nearly ten years now, he'd been picking up freelance gigs from newspapers and organizations all over the world. He never turned down anything that meant travel and adventure. He specialized in exotic locales, endangered animals, and environmental catastrophes—with the occasional war zone thrown in just to spice things up.

It was a fun, satisfying lifestyle. Or it had been, but lately something felt different. As he jogged across the street in the last second of the walk signal, he wondered if it had to do with his brother's changing life. He shared an apartment with Colin when he was in town, but now that Colin was serious about Savannah, Chase didn't feel as free to show up unannounced. He didn't begrudge his brother his happiness, but all that cooing and canoodling made it tough to flop down on the couch with a beer and mindlessly watch *Ice Road Truckers* or *Swamp People*.

He missed hanging out with his brother. And now he was wondering if he should start knocking on his own apartment door before entering ever since he'd caught Colin and Savannah in a compromising position on the living room floor. He'd been trying to erase the image from his brain ever since.

He turned the corner and saw Sweet Happens up ahead, but his mind was somewhere else and he almost forgot why he was there. Thinking about Colin and Savannah inevitably led him to Rayne. And her mesmerizing gray eyes, her sweet face framed by waves of chocolate-brown hair, and the slender curves that suited the slightly hippie clothes she wore. There was a goodness about her but a worldliness, too, and Chase found the whole package nearly irresistible.

He would have asked her out long ago, but his brother had told Chase to steer clear of her. Colin said Rayne wanted someone who was stable and predictable, and Chase was neither of those things. He couldn't argue with that or with Colin's obvious desire to keep their circle of friends on good terms, and yet he couldn't fully let go of the attraction. But whenever he thought about asking her out anyway, something stopped him. And it wasn't just because of all the concerns Colin had raised. It was an odd sort of shyness he hadn't felt around women in years.

As he pushed open the door to Sweet Happens, the owner, Crystal, looked up from behind the counter with a big smile on her face. Chase smiled back. It was late afternoon, and there were a smattering of stay-at-home moms with kids in strollers and a couple of young black-clad Goths trying to look suitably alienated while they ate cupcakes with pink frosting.

"Chocolate-filled croissant?" Crystal asked, handing him a coffee mug.

"Sure," Chase said and then suddenly wondered whether his ordering pattern qualified him as predictable enough to ask Rayne out. He filled the mug with hazelnut coffee from the self-serve station by the counter while Crystal put the croissant on a plate. He starting digging in his pocket for money, but she shook her head.

"On the house," she said.

"Thanks!" He thought about taking his laptop outside, but it was too damn hot. He swore the jungles of Vietnam had nothing on D.C. in August. "You have free Wi-Fi, right?"

Crystal shook her head. "Sorry, I can't afford that."

"Damn. I need to send some emails. I suppose I could use my cell phone."

He balanced the coffee mug on the plate with the pastry and was turning toward a table in far corner when Crystal said,

"There's an exhibit of Roger Thaw's photography opening at the National Geographic building next week."

Chase looked at her over his shoulder. Colin had told him that Crystal was still hung up on him after their brief fling several months ago, even though Chase had taken off for an overseas assignment in mid-fling and stayed away from Sweet Happens for weeks after he'd gotten back to town.

"I managed to get tickets to the opening reception," Crystal said. "It's pretty exclusive. I asked a friend of mine to go with me, but she's got to go out of town, so...would you want to go? I mean, it would strictly be as friends."

In his experience, women never meant it when they said that. "Let me check my schedule and see if I'll be in town, OK?"

"Sure, yeah, that would be fine. It's not till next Thursday, so maybe let me know by Tuesday?"

"Yeah, OK. And thanks again," he said, holding the plate a little higher. "I appreciate it."

He didn't want to give Crystal the wrong idea, but he did enjoy her company and the reception would be a great opportunity for him to do some networking. He had a serious itch to get out of the country, but he was having trouble drumming up an assignment. Washington came to a standstill as the summer wound down. With Congress and half the federal workforce on vacation, activity all but stopped. He needed to tap into some farther-flung contacts, and those New York editors might just come to D.C. for an opening of a show by nature photographer Roger Thaw.

Plus, Crystal did have a sweet-ass figure, and he'd always like the artsy, slightly exotic vibe she gave off—and her lean, muscular body and that little tattoo of a butterfly on her left hip, just above the panty line...

"Focus, man," he said under his breath. He set his coffee and pastry on the small table, pulled his phone out of his back pocket, and sat down. He scrolled through the list of editors he'd worked with before and typed out a series of emails with the same basic message: *Looking for an assignment. Got anything going on?*

He sipped his coffee and checked BBC News on his phone, looking to see where the hot spots were. He was steering clear of the Middle East for the time being. That shit was too unpredictable even for him.

If he didn't find something soon, he was going to face serious pressure from his father. He'd already spent the past week deflecting his mother's phone calls to come to their house in Georgetown and take photos of her garden. He normally didn't mind doing that, but it inevitably meant crossing paths with his father, who constantly asked when Chase was going to give up this ridiculous vagabond lifestyle and get a real job—which meant managing one of the family's many restaurants and bars in the D.C. metro area. Colin was good at it and so was their sister Jessica. But Chase would be a disaster, and he couldn't believe his father didn't see it. Never mind how miserable his son would be—surely his father wouldn't want to bring that kind of dishonor on the company.

Around 6:00, he texted Colin: *Yo, bro! Where you hanging tonight?*

He grabbed his shoulder bag and was returning his dishes to the counter when Colin texted back: *Zipped for awhile, then B&B. Like usual.*

Chase waved goodbye to Crystal as he pushed open the door with his shoulder and texted Colin back: *Headed your way! Put in an order of wings for me!*

When he got to Zipped, the place was half full of office workers stopping off for a drink before heading home. The bar was usually packed on Thursdays for trivia night, but Colin didn't bother with it in August because there weren't enough regulars in town. Chase went straight to the bar, where Savannah was sitting. Colin saw him coming and turned around to grab a bottle of tequila and a shot glass. He poured the drink and slid it over to Chase then pulled out of bottle of Landshark lager and stuck a wedge of lime in the bottle.

"God bless your superpower," Chase said. He downed the tequila and set the glass down on the bar with a satisfying thunk. "Exactly what I needed."

Savannah had a plate of half-eaten chicken wings in front of her, and Chase eyed it hungrily. She drank the last of her soda and grabbed her bag.

"I've got an early meeting tomorrow so I'm going to head home," she said. "I'll just say goodbye to Rayne before I go."

Chase had already grabbed a chicken wing off the plate and now he paused with it in midair. "Rayne's here?" he said.

"Yes, Rayne's here!" Rayne sang out from behind him.

He turned and saw her walking over from the direction of the bathrooms. Her face was flushed a pretty shade of pink, and she swayed a little as she walked.

Savannah slid off her barstool. "I'm going home," she said to Rayne. "But I want to talk more about your work thing."

"I'll come with you," Rayne said, reaching for her purse.

"You don't have to cut your night short just because I am. Stay and eat. Seriously."

Rayne leaned closer to Savannah and lowered her voice but not enough that Chase couldn't help hearing, "I didn't eat lunch, and that margarita went right to my head."

"Yeah, I noticed," Savannah said. "But don't worry about work. I'm sure Jeremy will figure something out. Oh and Chase," she said as she slung her bag over her shoulder, "I'm sleeping at my house tonight, so you and Colin can have some quality time together."

Chase turned to Colin in open-mouthed surprise. "I never said I wanted quality time."

Colin laughed. "You didn't have to. The way you've been moping around the apartment or holed up in your room, it's pretty obvious."

Savannah shook her head, smiling, and leaned over the bar to give Colin a kiss. As she walked away, Rayne slid onto the barstool next to Chase and drank the last few drops of her drink, then rattled the ice cubes and peered into the glass as though hoping for more. She was wearing a sleeveless dress that hugged her waist and flared out at the hips. It was flattering, and he thought about telling her so but took a swig of his beer instead.

"What is it you're not supposed to worry about?" he asked.

"I'm not supposed to even talk about it," Rayne said. "I only told Savannah because I tell her everything. Well, not *everything*, but I had to tell someone."

She tucked her hair behind her ear and shifted in her seat—and nearly slid off the barstool. Chase reached out to steady her, but she grabbed the edge of bar and righted herself. His hand hovered in the air for a few seconds as he wondered whether he could touch her anyway without being obvious, but as soon as he hesitated, he felt as awkward as a teenager, and he let his hand drop.

Colin brought a plate of cranberry and brie crostinis and set it down in front of Rayne.

"Eat!" he said.

"Can I have another margarita, please?" she asked, holding up her glass.

"Eat something first and then we'll talk," Colin said.

"Yessir!" Rayne said and saluted.

Chase and Colin laughed, and Rayne giggled. She was adorable when she giggled.

Colin moved off down the bar, and Rayne reached across Chase to pick up one of the wings. She bit into it, and sauce smeared her cheeks. He shifted in his seat, fighting the urge to find out how the sauce tasted on her skin.

"They're spicy tonight," she said, finally brushing a napkin across her mouth.

"Yeah," he said, and his voice was hoarse.

She bit into one of the crostinis. "These are sweet. Which do you like better: spicy or sweet?"

He took a long drink of his beer. "It depends."

"Sometimes I like both at the same time. That's why barbecue sauce works."

"And General Tso's chicken," he said, starting to feel buzzed and wishing they could talk about something less sensual—and at the same time wishing she'd never stop.

"Oh, and Mexican hot chocolate."

Colin came around from behind the bar. "What are you guys

talking about?" he asked, giving Chase a look he chose to ignore.

"Spicy or sweet?" Rayne said. "Which do you like better?"

"Sweet," Colin said. "But if salty's in the mix, I might have to reconsider. Right now, though, I'm heading to Balance&Bite." He turned to Chase. "See you back at our place later?"

"Sure, bro. I'll pick up some beer on the way home," Chase said.

Colin headed for the door, and Chase was turning back to the bar when a man walked over to him.

"Hey, Chase," the man said.

"Hey, Ben. Good to see you." They shook hands, and Chase gestured to Rayne. "This is my friend Rayne. Care to join us?"

Ben nodded at Rayne and said, "Nah, I'm with some co-workers. We just stopped in for a quick beer. We're on deadline tonight."

"Ben's managing editor of D.C. magazine," Chase said to Rayne.

"That's a great magazine," Rayne said. "I read it all the time."

"Thanks," Ben said with a smile, then he motioned to Diana, a waitress who sported pink hair and multiple ear piercings, and ordered a Sam Adams draft. Rayne asked for a margarita.

"I got your email but didn't get a chance to respond," Ben said to Chase. "I might have something for you."

"Oh yeah?" Chase perked up immediately.

"It's not my gig to assign, but I know a guy who's looking for someone to do a piece on Nepal after the earthquake. He's lining up a writer, but he wanted to send a photographer, too. Someone with experience in places like that."

Chase pulled his cell phone out of his pocket. "Do you have his number?"

"Not on me. Let me talk to my contact first, and if it looks good, I'll send you the info."

Diana brought his beer, and Ben laid some money on the bar and picked up the glass. "It's a new magazine, and I hear the financing is pretty solid, but I want to check it out first. I wouldn't want to send you halfway around the world for something that's not the real deal."

"I appreciate that, man," Chase said. "But you know me, halfway around the world is never a bad deal."

Ben took a drink of his beer and shook his head with a smile. "Yeah, for a second, I forgot who I was talking to." Then he turned to Rayne. "Nice meeting you."

Rayne waved and turned her attention to the margarita Diana had just brought her. She drank half of it in one swallow. Chase slid his phone back into his pocket and said, "Whoa! Maybe you should slow down!"

"I've been to Nepal," she said.

He was surprised. "You have?" According to Savannah and Colin, Rayne was a definite homebody.

"Mmm-hmmm. When I was about twelve, my parents took me all around Nepal and India. I think I still have the sari they bought me."

"That's a hell of a summer vacation."

She fiddled with the edge of the napkin under her drink, which was wet with condensation. "We didn't really take vacations. I mean, not in the normal sense. My parents were kind of hippies so we moved around. A lot. Sometimes we went to exotic places and stayed there for a while, or not. It just depended."

He took the last swig of his beer, watching her. "Sounds like you didn't enjoy it."

"Oh, it was fine, but I'm happy to stay put now." She took another sip of her drink. "So you just go wherever someone sends you?"

"Pretty much. That way, when I'm upset with my boss, I find a new one instead of drowning my sorrows in margaritas," he said with a wink.

She gazed at him. Her cheeks had gone a little pinker, and her smoky gray eyes looked serious. "I guess I am drowning my sorrows, but I'm not upset with my boss. Well, maybe a little. He wants to shut down the organization because of one setback, and I think he's giving up too quickly."

"You work for a conservation outfit, right?" Chase asked, hoping he was remembering correctly. He was rewarded with a look of surprise and a nod. She obviously thought he hadn't been paying that much attention. Or else she was remembering his mostly deserved reputation for messing up the details, which had nearly cost Colin his relationship with Savannah.

"Global climate change," Rayne said, finishing her drink and signaling to Diana for another. Chase gave Diana his own signal and watched as she poured only a dash of tequila into the drink. She also brought Chase another beer.

"But it doesn't really matter because we're losing the building," Rayne said. Then she turned toward him, and the words came tumbling out. "Our office is in this awesome old house on the Hill, but we're just leasing it and the landlord wants to convert it into condos and we can't afford to go anywhere else. Or at least that's what Jeremy says. And now this amazing organization is going to fold and I'm going to lose a job I love."

She stopped to catch her breath, and her eyes went wide. "It's supposed to be a secret." She put her hand on Chase's arm and tightened her fingers around his wrist. "Please don't tell anyone."

Chase looked down at her hand. Her fingers were pressing against his pulse, and the throbbing sensation made it hard for him to focus.

"Promise me," she said, and she had such an intent look of concern on her face that he immediately said, "Yeah, sure, I won't tell anyone."

She relaxed and let go of his arm, and he wished he hadn't agreed so quickly. He took a long drink of his beer and said, "Maybe there's some way you guys could raise the money to buy the place."

"I was thinking about that, but our fundraising director is on maternity leave."

"Maybe you could do it."

"Me? I don't know the first thing about raising money."

He shrugged. "What's to know? You're passionate about the organization, and it sounds like you care about the old house. The rest is just logistics. You could figure it out."

She stared at him dumbfounded for a moment then a little smile started to lift the corners of her mouth. She pulled her phone out of her purse and keyed in her password, and he watched a photo of a bird pop up on her screen. Then she opened on a note-taking app and typed: *Hold a fundraiser. Me?*

"A blue-footed booby?" he asked, pointing to the bird on her phone.

She looked up at him in surprise. "Not many people know what it is. I love that bird. The silly blue feet. And the name. It makes me giggle." Which she did. And he wished like hell he had the nerve to kiss her. If she was any other woman, he would have already done that and more.

She took a ten out of her wallet and slid it under the plate. "They never let me pay here because of Savannah, but would you make sure Diana gets this?"

"Of course," Chase said. "Are you taking off?"

"Yeah, it's been a long day, and I'm starting to crash. I'll see you around."

He wanted to ask if he could walk her home or take her to dinner sometime or skip all that and go straight to bed, but he seemed to have completely lost his game.

"Sure thing," he said.

While he was finishing his beer and checking his phone for messages, Diana came over to clear away the dishes. She found the ten Rayne had left.

"Since when did you become such a big tipper?" she asked.

"Rayne left it." He was disappointed to see that only a couple of his contacts had responded and the answers were all no, nothing going on right now. He hoped Ben's lead would turn into something substantial.

Diana picked up Rayne's napkin and uncovered a cell phone.

"I take it this isn't your phone," she said. "Unless you carry a spare."

He picked up the phone and pressed the button to light up the screen. There behind the password keypad was the photo of the blue-footed booby.

"It's Rayne's," he said.

Diana reached to take it from him. "I'll put it in the lost and found," she said.

"No," Chase said, a little more sharply than he'd intended. "I'll get it back to her."

Diana eyed him suspiciously, but he pretended not to notice. "Suit yourself," she said.

Chase headed for the door, still holding the phone. It was smaller than his, and it fit nicely in his palm. He was smiling when he stepped out onto the sidewalk, ridiculously pleased to have a reason to see her again, away from Zipped and his brother's disapproving looks. Of course, he'd have to figure out where she lived first.

Chapter 3

The next morning, Rayne woke up with a raging headache and a mouth so dry she couldn't have spit if her life depended on it. Though she couldn't imagine a situation when that would be necessary. She stumbled to the bathroom and gulped down some aspirin then headed downstairs to the kitchen. She heated water for tea and threw a couple slices of bread in the toaster. As Rayne was smearing butter and jam on the toast, Savannah walked in, already dressed for work.

"So how long did you stay at Zipped last night?" Savannah asked as she rinsed out her coffee mug in the sink. "I completely conked out as soon as I got home so I didn't even hear you come in."

"I didn't stay too much longer," Rayne said, taking a sip of her tea. She knew what Savannah was really asking and figured there was no point in being coy. "Chase and I talked for awhile and then I walked myself home."

Savannah looked relieved. She didn't want Rayne dating Chase any more than Colin did. Rayne knew they were just trying to look out for her, but it still made her feel like a child—or fragile, which she didn't like either. Chase had a reputation for romancing women and then taking off for parts unknown when things got complicated or boring. But she had really enjoyed hanging out with him, and even when she woke up, she still had a warm feeling.

She was starting to think the risk of a little heartbreak was worth the chance to cuddle up to that body, run her hands through his hair, pull his ruggedly handsome face close to hers....

Rayne suddenly realized that Savannah was watching her with a puzzled expression. She gobbled down the last of her toast. "I've got to get ready for work," she said. "But will you be around tonight?"

Savannah nodded. "Yeah, I've been so busy that I'm really looking forward to vegging out on the couch."

They walked into the living room together, and Savannah grabbed her bag and keys.

"I'll stop by Sweet Happens on my way home and get us something yummy to munch on," Rayne said.

"You read my mind!" Savannah said and headed out the door.

Rayne took a quick shower and put on a sleeveless dress of silky green. Then she remembered Chase's idea about a fundraiser and wanted to check her phone to see if she'd made any notes about it. Aside from remembering how absolutely yummy Chase had looked, the previous night was a bit of a blur. She dug through her purse but couldn't find her phone, and it wasn't plugged into the charger. Rayne turned her bedroom upside down looking for her phone, but the only interesting thing she found was the sari her parents had bought her in India, the one she'd mentioned to Chase last night. She smiled and immediately wanted to tell him about it, but then remembered that she didn't have her phone. And didn't know his number anyway.

She checked the whole house, but her phone was nowhere to be found. She was starting to feel panicky without it, but she was already late for work. As she raced down the porch steps, she wondered if she'd left it at the office. But no, she distinctly remembered pulling it out when she was talking to Chase.

As she walked, she kept an eye on the sidewalk in case it had fallen out of her purse, but no luck. She must have left it at Zipped. At least it would be safe there, and she could pick it up on her way home from work. But that meant a whole day without her notes or text messages or phone calls. Her panicky feeling intensified. What if there was an emergency? She tried to calm her nerves by telling herself she could call Zipped when it opened at lunchtime and confirm that it was there.

But when she called, Colin said he hadn't seen the phone and it wasn't in the lost-and-found box. To add to her frustration, Jeremy was out of the office all day so she couldn't talk to him about what they could do to save the organization. She finally managed to get some work done by pretending that Jeremy was handling the situation and everything was back to normal.

Chase woke up that morning to the sound of his phone ringing. He looked at the caller ID with bleary eyes.

"Hey, Mom," he said when he answered.

"Hi, honey. I was hoping you could come by today and take some photos. And maybe stay for lunch?"

He glanced at the clock. Nine a.m. "Sure thing, but give me an hour or so to get my gear together."

"Excellent! See you soon."

He stumbled out of his bedroom and found Colin already showered and dressed and heading for the door. He and Chase had drunk beer and watched TV till the wee hours of the morning, like old times, and Chase had thoroughly enjoyed himself. But he'd had to turn off the ringer on Rayne's phone because it kept beeping with text messages, and he didn't want Colin to know he had it.

He had resisted the urge to hold onto the phone and try to catch the messages as they came in. It was none of his business and way too creepy. But he couldn't help wondering whether it was a guy—or guys—trying to get hold of her.

"Do you ever even get a chance to sleep?" Chase said to Colin as he walked into the kitchen in his boxers and T-shirt and grabbed a box of cereal and a bowl. "Our old man's got you working like a dog."

"I'm not working for him," Colin said, scooping up his keys from the table by the door. "I'm working for myself. And you know, a little hard work wouldn't kill you."

Chase poured milk over his cereal and sat down on the couch to eat. "I work my ass off when I'm on an assignment. When it's time to relax, I relax."

"I'll just have to take your word for the hard work part. You've got the relaxing down to a fine art."

Chase waved. "Enjoy your day at the office, honey!"

He finished his cereal and was digging out some clean clothes before jumping in the shower when Rayne's phone buzzed and skittered a little on his nightstand. He grabbed it to keep it from falling on the floor and saw a text message scroll across the top of the screen. It was from someone named Eric. *Not sure you got my other messages. At hospital with Ada. Will text again after I talk to the doctor.*

Chase took a taxi over to Georgetown, and when he walked into the house, his mom had holly draped over the fireplace and was wearing a long black skirt and a red sweater with a snowflake pattern around the collar. It was ninety degrees out.

"You didn't say anything about Christmas card pictures," Chase said. "I don't have the right lights with me."

"Whatever you do, I'm sure it will be fine," she said, kissing him on the cheek. "This was the only morning your father could do it, and I already had Maria give Regina a bath."

"Ma, no one will be able to tell if the dog stinks in a photograph," he said as he started pulling equipment out of his duffel bag. He was setting up a portable light when a black Labrador came bounding over. She had a red velvet ribbon tied in a big bow around her neck. He crouched down to scratch her behind the ears and was rewarded with a lick across the face.

"Who's a good dog?" Chase asked, and Regina danced back and forth and wagged her tail so hard he thought she'd take off like a helicopter.

His father came into the room, fastening his gold cufflinks as he walked. "Glad you could take time out of your busy schedule to come by," he said.

Chase rose to his feet. "Nice to see you, too, Pops," he said with a smile. "Looks like I'm not the only one who can't say no to Mom."

His father was dressed in one of his best black suits—though all his suits were expensive and perfectly tailored to his tall, lean figure—and he had on a red tie flecked with gold accents.

"Touché," his father said, and his expression softened. "I

don't have time this morning because I need to get to the office as soon as this photo shoot is done, but I'd like to talk to you about—"

"Please don't say 'my future,' Dad," Chase said, turning away to set up his tripod.

"I'm having trouble finding a general manager for one of my new properties," his father said. "I think it would suit you."

"Nothing about the restaurant industry 'suits' me," Chase said. Then he smiled. "Except maybe the free food."

His father's face went dark. "You're thirty-two years old, son. It's past time for you to be settling down into some sort of steady employment. Something with a future."

"A future of what?" Chase asked, trying not to take his frustration out on his expensive equipment. They'd been having this argument for ten years, and his father had never even tried to see his point of view. Chase's grandfather had built the business, and his father had grown up in it so he knew no other life, but Chase did. "A future of being stuck in this town working fourteen-hour days till I die?"

"There's nothing wrong with hard work," his father said. "What do you think paid for you to go to college?"

"Boys!" Chase's mother said. "Could you save this argument for later? It's Christmas."

Chase wanted to say he'd be happy to save it till doomsday.

His mother bustled around getting his father into position in front of the fireplace. Then she sat down in the gold damask armchair, smoothed out her skirt, and called the dog to her. Regina, who'd been sniffing around Chase and his camera equipment, instantly ran to her side and sat down facing the camera, head up, tail still.

Chase adjusted his camera, switched on his light, and turned off the room lights. There was just the right glow around his parents' faces. He had to admit his mother had put everything together well. There was a nice balance of textures and colors— the stone of the fireplace, the sharp green of the holly leaves, the black and red with a touch of gold in his parents' clothes.

He took a series of photos from different angles as quickly

as he could because his father started getting restless within minutes, and that sort of impatience could show through. He wanted his mother to have a nice selection to choose from for their Christmas cards, which she sent out by the hundreds—to friends and neighbors, employees and suppliers, fellow board members of the numerous charities she worked with. For all he knew, she sent cards all the way up to the Oval Office.

As soon as Chase was done, his father went upstairs to change into something more suitable for August, and his mother brought Chase a glass of lemonade.

"Hey, Ma, do you know a nonprofit group on Capitol Hill that works on climate change?" he asked as he packed up his equipment.

His mother was taking down the holly from the mantel, and Chase was surprised to realize it was fake. It looked so real. But of course, finding fresh holly this time of year was a trick that might be beyond even her skills.

"I believe the Center for Action on Climate Change is on Capitol Hill. Jeremy Banks runs it. He's a charming young man—and not hard to look at either," she said, and Chase looked up at her in open-mouthed surprise. "I met him last month at a party—I can't remember whose now—and we had a long conversation about the environment. He's very passionate about it."

"That's sounds like the place."

"Are you looking for work?" she asked.

He frowned at her. "Don't you start on me, too."

She put her hand up to stop him. "That's not what I meant. I thought you were interested in a photography assignment, because of the work they do. Whether you want to be a GM at one of our restaurants is between you and your father."

"Thanks," he said. "And I didn't have work in mind. I was talking to this girl the other night at Zipped, and she left her phone behind. I'm trying to get it back to her."

"A girl?" His mother raised her eyebrows and smiled hopefully.

"Yes, Ma, a girl. I do talk to them from time to time. Or

women, I should say. Isn't that more appropriate?"

"And this girl—ah, woman—works at Jeremy's organization?"

"I think so."

He finished packing up his equipment and was setting his bag by the door when his mother came back and handed him a business card. He glanced down and saw "Jeremy Banks, President" and contact info.

"Try the main number," his mother said. "You're staying for lunch, right? Maria made some of that chicken salad you like, with walnuts and grapes. And we've got peach pie and ice cream for dessert."

Chase grinned. "How could I resist? Just let me make this phone call first."

His mother went into the kitchen, and Chase dialed the number on the business card. He got an assistant of some sort—a competent woman with a silky smooth voice—who told him that yes, indeed, Rayne Michael worked there. She put him through to her extension, and his heart started beating a little faster in anticipation—and nerves. It was an unfamiliar, uncomfortable sensation.

He heard her saying, "This is Rayne Michael," and for a split second, his mind went blank, then he pulled himself together and said, "Hey, Rayne. It's Chase Allison."

She paused. "Chase? How did you... I mean, this is a surprise. Did I give you my work number? I have to admit that my mind is a little hazy on the details last night."

He laughed. "I thought that was more tequila than you were used to." He realized it might sound a little stalkerish to say he'd tracked her down through his mother, so he came up with a quick lie. "No, I remembered you mentioning the name of your organization."

"Oh, OK." She paused. "Is something wrong? Is Colin OK?" Her voice started to rise. "Did something happen to Savannah?"

"They're fine, they're both fine," he said quickly.

He heard a rustling sound and then Rayne saying something to someone else, though it was muffled. "I have to go into a meeting," she said. "So I need to keep this short."

He cleared his throat, fighting that awkward feeling again. "I was just calling to tell you that I've got your cell phone."

"You do!" He heard a soft thud as though she'd dropped something on her desk. "I've been going out of my mind without it! Where did you find it?"

"You left it at Zipped. I thought I could swing by your place tonight and drop it off. If you'll be around."

"That's sweet, but I don't want to put you out. You could leave it at Zipped and I could pick it up there."

"It's no problem. I'll be in the neighborhood anyway," he lied. "But you'll have to give me your address because I only have a general idea of where you live."

"Of course." She told him, and he jotted it down on a scrap of paper. "I should be home by 6."

"Great. I'll stop by sometime after."

He was thinking that if everything went smoothly, he could ask her to go for a drink and see where things went from there. Maybe they could have a late, casual dinner together, someplace not owned by Allison Inc. Colin's warnings be damned—there was something about this woman, and Chase thought there was no harm in a little reconnaissance.

"I've got to go," she said. "You're a lifesaver! Thanks a bunch."

He took a moment to key her address into his phone, and he was grinning like an idiot.

Chapter 4

Rayne's spirits lifted at the thought of Chase stopping by that evening, and she hoped the excitement would carry her through her meeting with Sheila and Jeremy. The landlord had told them he wasn't interested in selling the building, and Rayne was grabbing her notebook and files to head downstairs for a strategy meeting when her phone buzzed again. She felt a flicker of dread that it was Chase telling her he had changed his mind and would leave her phone at Zipped after all.

But it wasn't Chase. It was Miss Ada's son Eric.

"Where the hell have you been?" he said with uncharacteristic gruffness. "I've been texting you since last night."

"I lost my cell phone," she said. "Is something wrong?"

"I stopped by my mom's house last night and found her on the bathroom floor. She was having trouble breathing so I called an ambulance."

"Oh my god," Rayne said, jumping up from her chair. "Is she all right? What hospital?"

Eric gave a little laugh and his voice softened. "Calm down! She's OK. The doctor said it's a mild case of pneumonia. I can bring her home tomorrow, and I'll stay with her for a while till she's back on her feet."

"I thought she didn't look good when I saw her yesterday morning," Rayne said. "I should have called you then. I'm so sorry you couldn't get hold of me last night."

"Relax, it's all under control. But I have to say it threw me when you didn't respond to my texts. It almost freaked me out more than finding Mom in that state. Made me realize how much she and I rely on you."

Rayne smiled, feeling slightly better. "I'll mobilize the troops and we'll make sure you and Ada have plenty to eat. Keep me posted, OK?"

"You bet! And thanks."

"Anything for you and Ada," she said, doubly glad that Chase was returning her phone that evening.

Chase joined his mom outside on the brick-paved patio, which was shaded from the sun and relatively cool for such a warm day. His father had already left for the office, so Chase and his mom ate and then whiled away the afternoon in conversation. She caught him up on all the neighborhood gossip and whose daughter was dating which inappropriate man and the politicking of her various nonprofit boards. And even though he realized it had only been a ruse to get him to the house, he dug out his camera again and took some photos of the gardens, which were fragrant with roses and heliotrope and the smell of boxwood baking in the sun.

It was after 4:00 when he finally got up to leave, wanting to catch a cab across town before rush-hour commuters swamped the streets and a fifteen-minute ride turned into an hour-long slog. He planned to stop at his apartment and drop off his camera equipment before he went to see Rayne. And maybe change his shirt. He wanted to look good but casual, and he pondered his options on the cab ride home. And shook his head at himself. He couldn't remember the last time he'd spend so much time agonizing over what to wear for a simple errand.

As he was getting ready, he checked his email. He wasn't making any progress on setting up a photo assignment, but he did have a message from one of his professional organizations about Roger Thaw's exhibit, which made him think of Crystal's offer. If he hadn't dated her—and broken her heart—he wouldn't hesitate to take her up on it. But he was feeling so upbeat about seeing Rayne that it made him confident that he could handle things with Crystal. Besides, he really needed to do some professional networking. He sent Crystal a quick text saying he'd go with her to the opening.

On the way home, Rayne stopped at the corner market to pick up some things so she could make lasagna for Ada and Eric, then she swung by Sweet Happens because she hadn't forgotten her promise to Savannah.

In the back of her mind was the happy thought that Chase would be stopping by, that he wanted to stop by rather than take the much easier route of simply leaving her phone at Zipped. It was a welcome boost that lifted the gloom she was feeling about work.

She walked into the shop and took a moment to savor the sweet smells of cakes baking. She could almost taste the sugar in the air.

"Hey, Rayne," Crystal said as she came out of the back room carrying a tray of cupcakes. "I just finished frosting these babies. Strawberry with a hint of lime. Want to try one?"

She handed Rayne a spoon with a scoop of frosting, and when Rayne tasted it, she nearly moaned with pleasure. "This is amazing," she said. "You are a true artist."

Crystal laughed. "Yeah, well, at least these generate income." She glanced at the far wall, and Rayne turned around to follow her gaze.

Hung on the wall were a series of framed watercolors of abstract flowers in vibrant fuchsia, hot pink, canary yellow, and tangerine. She'd never seen such brilliantly painted watercolors. They were energizing and oddly soothing at the same time.

"Are those yours?" Rayne asked, walking over to take a closer look.

"Yes. I thought maybe if I hung a few in here, I might generate some interest, maybe even make a sale or two."

"They're gorgeous," Rayne said. "How long have you been doing this?"

"I started painting in high school. I was always doodling and sketching, but then I discovered watercolor and went to the art school at the Corcoran, where I had a fantastic teacher." Crystal came out from behind the counter, wiping her flour-covered hands on her apron. "She taught me so much about color and just opening yourself up to life and whatever's inside you, just letting that beauty out. I've been trying to get into a gallery, but it helps to have some sales first."

Crystal joined her, and Rayne eyed the small, tasteful price tags, but at $300 apiece, she couldn't afford to splurge on one.

"I dabble in photography, too," Crystal said, "but watercolor's my main thing. Though I did get tickets to the opening of Roger Thaw's show the other night. I swear some of his photos of water are like paintings."

"Oh, I've heard of him. In fact, we've used some of his photos on our website at work."

"He's got an amazing eye for photography."

"He's not bad looking either," Rayne said with a grin.

Crystal blushed. "I am aware of that, but I actually asked someone to go with me. I told him it's not a date, but I'm still hoping."

"Oh?"

"We had a thing for awhile, but then he took off on an overseas assignment—his way of ending things when they got too hot to handle, in my opinion."

"And were things that serious?" Rayne asked, following Crystal back to the counter.

Crystal smiled. "I like to think so."

"Well, I hope it works out for you—with your paintings and the guy," Rayne said, scanning the display case and trying to decide whether to take Savannah a chocolate-frosted cupcake or a strawberry one.

"I think Chase and I are a good match," Crystal said. "I just have to get him to see it that way."

Rayne's heart jumped ahead a beat. "Chase?"

"Chase Allison, Colin's brother. You know him, right—because of Savannah?"

Crystal turned to get a white bakery box from the shelf so Rayne had a moment to recover. "Sure. Of course."

"So what can I get you?"

Rayne was still flustered, but she hid it by pretending to ponder her options. "Give me three of the strawberry cupcakes and three chocolates."

Crystal boxed up the cupcakes, and Rayne handed her cash. Crystal was counting out change when her cell phone beeped. The sound made Rayne long for her own phone.

Crystal dug the phone out of her pocket to check the text message. "Yes!" she said. Then she looked up at Rayne, her eyes glowing with excitement. "Chase said yes. He'll go to the opening with me."

Chase walked up the steps to Rayne's front porch around 7:00, wearing jeans and a short-sleeved, button-down cotton shirt he'd gotten in Bali. It was still light out, but it was overcast, and without the sun beating down, the heat felt slightly less oppressive. Chase knocked on the front door, and seconds later, Rayne pulled it open, a little out of breath. She had a dish towel in her hand and a streak of what looked like tomato sauce on her cheek.

"Hey!" she said.

"Hey." He gestured toward her face. "You've got something..."

"Oh!" She scrubbed at her cheek with the dish towel and looked at him with a question in her eyes. Those smoky, smoldering eyes. Like a stormy sky. It made him wonder what sort of pent-up passion was hidden behind those eyes.

He realized he'd kept her waiting and said, "Yeah, all good now."

A timer dinged somewhere inside the house, and she turned toward the sound then back to him. "Come in for a second. I'm in the middle of making lasagna. That's why I'm such a mess."

He wanted to tell her that she wasn't a mess. In fact, he liked the slightly distracted, tousled look. It made him think about her in bed. But he kept his thoughts to himself and followed her into the kitchen. Rayne took the lid off a pot of noodles and stirred, then turned off the heat and reached for a rectangular glass dish.

"I didn't know you were into cooking," he said.

"I'm not really. I'd usually just as soon eat out. Probably because I didn't get to do much of that when I was a kid.

Thankfully, my mom is a fantastic cook. But every once in awhile I get the urge to make something."

She bustled around the kitchen getting sauce, cheese, and sautéed meat and veggies together.

"Whatever you're doing, it smells delicious," he said.

"This is my go-to recipe when I need something for a sick friend."

He suddenly remembered the text message. "Ada?"

She looked up at him in surprise. "How did you know?"

He was embarrassed and tried to hide it by digging her cell phone out of his pocket. "I happened to be picking up your phone when a text message came in. I wasn't spying, honest!"

She wiped her hands on the towel, took the phone from him, and punched in her password.

"That thing has been going off the entire time I had it," he said. "You must have forty-seven text messages by now."

"Seventeen," she said with a smile. "Mostly from Ada's son saying—" Rayne paused as she skimmed through the messages— "he was taking her to the hospital. She's got a mild case of pneumonia. Not life-threatening but serious enough for someone her age."

She set the phone down and started layering cheese and noodles and all the fillings into the large pan and another smaller one. "He got hold of me at work today and told me he's bringing her home this evening. He's going to stay with her for a few days until she's feeling better. Hence, the lasagna."

Chase watched her, savoring the smells of home cooking and trying to remember the last time he'd had a meal made by his mother, not Maria. He ate out at restaurants so often that sharing a home-cooked meal was starting to sound like the sexiest date ever.

Someone knocked on the door, and Rayne went to answer it. While he was waiting, he noticed a box on the counter with the distinctive brown and teal Sweet Happens logo on it and felt a twinge of something like guilt. Colin accused Chase of being a player because he rarely stayed with any woman for long. But however brief his flings, he was a one-woman man once things got underway. Seeing Crystal's logo made him feel like he was cheating. And though he wasn't sure who he was supposed to be cheating on, it wasn't a feeling he liked.

Rayne came back a few minutes later with a covered casserole dish. "The woman next door wants me to take this to Ada's house when I go," she explained as she set the dish on the counter.

"Do you do this a lot—take care of your neighbors?" Chase asked.

Rayne put the final layer of sauce and noodles in the pans. "I don't know if it's a lot, just whenever it's needed I guess."

Chase scooped up a leftover slice of zucchini and popped it in his mouth. "When I was growing up, we knew our neighbors, but in a formal sort of way. Never well enough to bake them lasagna when they were sick."

"Maybe it's my upbringing," she said. "We always lived in these out-of-the-way, off-the-grid places, and everyone had to look out for each other. Self-reliance only goes so far."

"I'm a big fan of self-reliance."

"Yeah, I noticed," she said under her breath, and he was pretty sure she hadn't meant him to hear. But he couldn't help grinning. So she'd noticed him?

Then he was distracted by the curve of her hips in her cutoff jean shorts and her lean, tanned legs as she bent forward to slide the pan into the oven. She closed the oven door, twisted the dial on a timer shaped like a ladybug, and turned to face him.

"It's too hot—wait, why are you smiling? Do I have something on my face again?" She swiped at her cheek with a dish towel.

"No! You look great," Chase said. He'd said it dozens of times to attractive women, and it usually netted him a smile and a flirtatious response. His grin faded, though, as Rayne gazed at him without saying anything.

"I was about to say it's too hot in here with the oven on," she finally said, "so I was going to sit on the porch while this bakes. Do you want to hang out for a while?"

"Sure," he said, relieved that she'd asked. Her look had been a little frosty, and it made him wonder what Colin might have told her about him.

One night last spring shortly after Chase had met her, he and Rayne had a little too much to drink and ended up snuggled together in a back booth at Zipped—until Colin and Savannah swept her away. Rayne hadn't been unfriendly after that, but she'd never mentioned it and never let him get that close again. Colin asked Chase to back off right after, and he assumed Savannah had given Rayne a similar warning.

Chase had gone on a photo assignment days later, and it helped him forget about her—for awhile at least. But he still thought about that night and how good it had felt to have her curled up next to him and how comfortable and unguarded she'd been with him.

Rayne was taking a pitcher out of the fridge. "Want some iced tea?" she asked. "I'll warn you that I make it pretty sweet."

"What about spicy?" he asked with a grin.

She laughed, and he was pleased to see that she remembered their conversation the night before. "I haven't figured out how to do that with tea."

She grabbed two glasses from the cupboard, poured the tea over ice, added some lemon slices, and handed him a glass. Then she grabbed the ladybug timer and her phone and led him out to the front porch. She sat down on the glider and he sat in the wicker chair.

He sipped the tea. She wasn't kidding about making it sweet, but the tea was strong and the lemon helped counter the sweetness. "So how are things at work?" he asked. "Have you given any more thought to that fundraising idea?"

Rayne pressed the glass of tea to her cheek, which was bright red from the heat of the kitchen. "I have," she said. "I'm not sure I can pull it off without our fundraising person, and we're having trouble getting the landlord to even talk to us about selling, but I was thinking we could do some sort of silent auction. Only what would we auction off?"

The answer came to him immediately. "What about photos and paintings of endangered animals and places?"

She gazed at him intently, but he wasn't sure whether she was actually seeing him or thinking about what he'd said. He gazed right back at her, glad to have the chance to openly watch her.

"An art auction? That is...an excellent idea!" she finally said. "I would just need to find enough really great stuff from some high-profile artists. And donors with lots of money to spend. Plus, we could reach out beyond the conservation community to people who support the arts. Maybe also tap the local art scene."

Her excitement was contagious—and she was damn sexy when she got fired up about something—so Chase didn't even pause to think about it before he said, "I could help with all those things."

She gazed at him again, but this time he was sure she was seeing him. A smile lit up her face, which he felt in his chest. Damn, this woman was good.

"You could? That would be awesome." She smiled at him and he would have sworn she was blushing, but it was hard to tell because her face was already flushed from the heat. She suddenly busied herself by tapping some notes into her phone.

"Maybe you could help me come up with a list of artists and then contact some of them...?" she said.

"Sure thing," Chase said with a smile. "Starting with myself, if that's OK."

"Of course!" Rayne said. "I've never seen your photos, but I'm sure they'd be perfect."

Part of him was thinking that this event would be a good opportunity to network for some new contacts and assignments. But another part of him was thinking that it would be a great excuse to spend time with her.

"I also know a lot of donor types, through my family," he said. "My mom is a wheeler-dealer in those circles. She could probably fill your event singlehandedly."

"I like her already," Rayne said with a smile. "I'm so glad you stopped by. I'm so glad I left my phone at Zipped last night! I'm going to put together a plan this weekend and then I'll talk to Jeremy—my boss—first thing Monday."

Chase was smiling back at her and thinking now would be

a good time to ask her to go for a drink when the screen door opened and Savannah stepped out onto the porch in shorts and a T-shirt, her long brown hair pulled back in a ponytail.

"Chase and I just came up with the best idea for saving CACC!" Rayne said.

Savannah looked at Chase, and he felt a chill. "Oh yeah?" she said.

"We're going to have a fancy event and auction off a bunch of photographs and paintings of animals and places that are threatened by climate change. Between my contacts and Chase's, we should be able to raise enough for a down payment on the house, assuming we can get Vincent to sell."

Savannah turned toward Rayne. "That's a terrific idea," she said. "Let me know what I can do to help."

"You know I will!" Rayne said. "Oh, and I'm making a small pan of lasagna for you."

"Aw, you take such good care of me!" Savannah said.

As far as Chase was concerned, the mood had been broken. "I need to go," he said. "But give me your number and I'll text you about scheduling a time to talk about this fundraiser."

Rayne gave him her number, and he keyed it into his phone.

"Thanks again!" she said. She picked up the empty iced tea glasses and went inside just as the ladybug timer dinged. Savannah started to follow but turned with her hand on the screen door and glared at Chase.

"Don't even think about making her one of your conquests," she said and let the door bang shut behind her.

Chapter 5

Rayne walked into the kitchen buzzing with excitement over the prospect of saving CACC—and doing it with Chase's help. As friends, she reminded herself as she pulled the lasagna pans out of the oven.

When Savannah walked in, Rayne said, "It will need to cool for a few minutes, but I'll have a piece for you in no time."

"Thanks," Savannah said, popping open the Sweet Happens box to peer inside. "What was Chase doing here?"

Rayne felt a little prickle of irritation, but she brushed it away. "He found my phone. I left it at Zipped the other night."

"Oh, that's excellent news!" Savannah said, closing the box and turning to face Rayne. "It was nice of him to bring it over, but, Rayney, maybe he's not the best person to work with on your fundraising idea. I mean, you know how...unpredictable he can be."

Rayne took a deep, calming breath. "I know that you're just looking out for me," she said. "But trust me, I've learned my lesson about getting involved with men who play around. And I'm feeling very grown up about this."

Savannah eyed her suspiciously. "What does that mean?" she asked.

"It means that I really need his help with this thing, and even though he's sexy as hell and I love hanging out with him, I can still have a professional relationship—maybe even a friendship—with him. Just like I do with Jeremy."

"Jeremy's a little different," Savannah said. "He's your boss. You don't run into him at bars, and he doesn't show up at your house on a Friday night."

Rayne sighed. "Yeah. And that's a pity." They both laughed. Rayne cut out a square of lasagna, put it on a plate with a fork, and handed it to Savannah. She took a bite and gave Rayne a thumbs-up.

"Besides, Chase is dating Crystal," Rayne said. "And I wouldn't want to mess that up for her."

Savannah had a mouthful of lasagna and had to chew and swallow before she could say, "Really? Colin told me that was over months ago."

"She asked him out, and he said yes, so I guess it's on again. She's an artist—did you know that? Watercolors mostly, and they are stunning." Rayne stopped. "I'm going to ask her to donate a painting for the auction. It would be awesome exposure for her. She's been trying to make a name for herself and get into a gallery."

She stuffed the oven mitts in a drawer and grabbed her phone off the counter. "I need to fire up my laptop and get all these ideas down while they're fresh. I'll join you for cupcakes later!"

In between visits to Miss Ada, Rayne spent most of the weekend writing up her strategy for the fundraiser and trying to anticipate Jeremy's questions. The only ones she couldn't answer were how much the landlord would want for the house—if he could be talked into selling it to CACC—and that meant she didn't know how much money they should aim to raise. She experimented with various dollar amounts until she was satisfied that she could address any concern Jeremy threw at her.

First thing Monday morning, she walked into his office and made her pitch. He listened thoughtfully, and when she was finished, he said, "You've done some excellent work. You've really thought this through."

She smiled, enjoying the praise and relieved that he'd let her go through her whole presentation despite the weary, skeptical look he'd given her when she walked in.

"The only hitch, of course," he said, "is getting Vincent to agree to sell to us. And that could be a big hitch."

Her heart started to sink. It sounded like he was saying no.

Jeremy gazed at the far corner of the room, idly drumming his fingertips on the desk. "I think the place to start would be getting the house appraised. Then I'll have Larry look into potential tax breaks for Vincent if he sells to a nonprofit—and the tax breaks for us, of course." As he talked, he pulled a notepad from the desk drawer. Rayne watched him carefully, barely able to breathe.

"As you said, we can't raise enough to buy it outright," he continued, "but perhaps a ten percent down payment could be our goal."

"So that's a yes?" Rayne asked.

He glanced up and smiled. "Yes, it's a yes. But we're not out of the woods yet. It's going to take a lot of work to pull this off."

"I know a great caterer who will probably give us a good deal," she said, knowing without a doubt that Colin would be on board. "And I was thinking we should have the event here. It would save us the cost of renting a place, and it makes sense for people to see the house they're saving."

"Brilliant!" He jotted down some more notes. "Give me time to do some brainstorming of my own and then let's bring the rest of the staff in on this and talk about it in more detail."

She nodded and got up to leave.

"And Rayne? Thank you for not letting me give up so easily."

He smiled that dazzling smile of his, and her knees went a little wobbly and she knew she was blushing like a schoolgirl. "Of course," she said with a smile and headed for the door.

"The photographer you mentioned—what was his name?" Jeremy asked.

She turned back to face him. "Chase Allison."

"Allison," he said, tapping his pencil on the pad. "I met a Beatrice Allison at a party awhile back. Charming woman, well connected. Family owns half the restaurants in town. Any relation?"

"Chase is her son," Rayne said. "His brother Colin is the guy I was thinking of asking to cater the event."

"She'd be a good woman to have in our corner. Nice work, Rayne. Email me a copy of your notes. And send Sheila in on your way out."

"Sure thing," Rayne said.

She found Sheila standing near the door. On the way in, Rayne had told her she wanted to talk to Jeremy about an idea to save the organization.

"Well?" Sheila asked anxiously.

Rayne gave her a big hug. "He wants to see you. And I bet you will look absolutely gorgeous in an evening gown!"

Sheila stared at her open-mouthed, but Rayne just smiled and flew up the stairs to her office.

Two days later, she was sitting at her desk munching on a salad as she tried to replicate the spreadsheet Savannah had created for her foundation's big donor event a few months ago. Rayne and Jeremy had decided to have CACC's gala on a Saturday six weeks away. It made for a tight schedule, but they needed to be sure they could raise enough money before the lease ran out at the end of November.

Once they committed to the fundraiser, Jeremy had told all the employees what was going on and everyone got an assignment, though Rayne was still in charge of the event, and happily so. She couldn't remember the last time she'd felt so energized, so focused.

She had talked to Colin that morning, and he had generously agreed to donate the food and charge them a reduced rate for the catering services. Next on her list was getting in touch with Chase about the artwork. But she didn't have his number. She picked up her phone to call Colin and ask for it and was startled when the phone beeped in her hand. She glanced at the number of the person texting her but didn't recognize it.

The message said: *So are we on for saving the planet?*

She smiled. Had to be Chase. She took a moment to jot down the number in a little notebook she'd started carrying around in case she ever lost her phone again. She didn't like feeling out of touch and especially hated that she hadn't known Miss Ada was in trouble.

Rayne texted back: *Yes! Got the ok from the boss. All systems are go! Congrats!*

Working like a fiend. Event is Oct 10!

We should have a planning meeting. I've got a list of photographers and online portfolios to show you. Sunday? Your place?

She was surprised—and a little thrilled—that he'd already gone to all that work without knowing whether the event would even happen. She was starting to think his reputation as a flake was unjustified.

She texted back: *You rock!! 1:00?*

Sure. Got any of that lasagna left?

Ha! It's long gone, but I can throw something together if we get hungry.

She was humming an aimless little tune as she put her phone away and went back to work. She was excited but didn't have that nervous, jittery feeling she usually got around men she was attracted to, which she took as a sign that her new grown-up approach was working.

On Sunday, Rayne tidied up the living room and cleared off the kitchen table. She'd debated cooking some sort of meal but wanted to keep things casual and didn't know how long he'd be staying anyway. She finally decided to have ingredients on hand to make sandwiches if the need arose.

Thunderstorms had rolled through the day before and broken the heat wave. The day was warm but comfortably so, and she was barefoot, wearing jeans and a sleeveless cotton blouse. She had purposely avoided fussing over her appearance. This wasn't a date after all—Chase was a colleague and a friend—but at the last minute, she couldn't resist dabbing on her favorite lily-of-the-valley perfume.

Chase showed up right at 1:00 with a laptop bag slung over his shoulder and a six-pack of Blue Moon beer in his hand.

"I figured we might get thirsty," he said as she opened the door.

"Great thinking." She started to lead him to the kitchen, but he motioned to the coffee table in the living room.

"Let's do it here. The light's better—too much glare in the kitchen."

She cleared a stack of magazines off the coffee table and

tried not to think about what it would be like to sit beside him on the couch. He set up his laptop while she took the beer into the kitchen. When she came back with two open bottles, she found him sitting on the floor with his back against the couch, scrolling through a website full of gorgeous photos of exotic places. As she handed him a beer, she felt a combination of relief and disappointment that he'd chosen the less cozy option of sitting on the floor.

She slid down next to him, careful not to sit too close, and he turned the laptop a little so she could see the screen easier.

"This is Roger Thaw's website," Chase said. "He would probably be the biggest name we could get. I met him the other night when I went to the opening of his show at the National Geographic headquarters." He took a swig of his beer. "I mentioned the auction to him, and he seemed interested. I just need to follow up with him."

In all the excitement, Rayne had forgotten about Chase's date with Crystal. She gave herself a mental pat on the back for it. Then she studied Thaw's photos—which were spectacular—and said, "Crystal mentioned something about getting tickets to that opening. It sounded pretty exclusive. Did you see her there?"

She didn't want to tell him she knew he'd gone with Crystal. It would imply that the two of them had been talking about him. And it might imply that Rayne cared who he went out with.

Chase paused for a moment. "Yeah, I did."

It wasn't the answer Rayne was expecting, and she was puzzled. But she decided to chalk his evasiveness up to a player's natural tendency to cover his tracks. Besides, she couldn't imagine doing this event without his help and contacts, and what he did with Crystal was none of her business.

For the next hour they sat side by side looking at breathtaking photographs of the Solomon Islands, the Maldives, Bangladesh, and the Great Barrier Reef. And heartbreaking images of polar bears clinging to melting chunks of ice, villages in Alaska slowly sinking into the thawing permafrost, starving people in the deserts of Darfur, retreating glaciers all over the world.

The beer was making Rayne feel fuzzy and relaxed, and the beautiful photos absorbed all her attention—until she leaned forward to see a detail Chase was pointing to. When her thigh pressed against his, the warmth of his body radiated through hers and ignited an explosion of desire that caused her to pull back as if she'd been shocked.

"You OK?" Chase asked turning his blue eyes on her, which made it even harder for Rayne to catch her breath.

"Yeah, I'm fine." She scrambled to her feet to put some distance between them and knocked over her empty beer bottle. She snatched it up before she could kick it across the floor, but the sudden movement made her feel lightheaded.

"You look a little flushed," Chase said. "You sure you're feeling OK?"

"It's just the beer," she said, taking a step backward toward the kitchen. "I'm thinking maybe I should have a bite to eat. Are you hungry?"

"I never say no to food," Chase said with a smile, "especially when it's not coming out of an industrial kitchen." He got to his feet and followed her into the kitchen.

"I can fix us some sandwiches," Rayne said as she opened the fridge. While she gathered the ingredients, she took the opportunity to remind herself that she was being a grown-up about all this.

She turned from the fridge with her arms full, and before she could protest, Chase took some of the things from her.

"Let me help," he said. "I'll let you do the hard work, though, because I'm really only skilled at peanut butter and jelly."

She laughed, finally starting to relax again. "Grab a couple plates out of that cupboard," she said, and when he did, she put slices of fresh ciabatta bread on each plate and layered organic chicken, avocado, lettuce, and tomato on top. Chase leaned a hip against the counter and watched her.

"Mustard or mayo?" she asked.

"Both," he said.

She added both to each sandwich, and he took two more beers out of the fridge.

"I was thinking we could eat on the porch and get some fresh air," he said, already moving toward the front door.

Rayne followed him out onto the porch. Chase took a bite of his sandwich and as soon as he'd chewed and swallowed said, "This is delicious. It might be the tastiest sandwich I've ever eaten."

Rayne laughed, pleased. "God, I hope that's not true! Your family runs the best restaurants in the city."

"Yeah, but they can't compete with fresh homemade food."

"I know what you mean," Rayne said. "I don't cook for myself so much, but it's fun to cook for—and with—other people. There's something very...communal about it. It makes me feel connected."

"And you like taking care of people," he said, half-statement, half-question.

"I guess so," she said, a little embarrassed because she'd just made him lunch and what did that say about her feelings?

As they ate and drank, they chatted about various details of the event. Then they watched the people coming and going from Eastern Market. She was thinking about India and how alive the streets always seemed, full of people and colors and the smells of cooking. Funny, she hadn't thought about that trip in years, not until she'd mentioned it to Chase.

"Reminds me of India," Chase said.

Rayne was startled—had he read her mind? "I was thinking the same thing."

He turned to look at her. "Great minds and all that," he said with a soft smile that only added to the intense connection she was feeling. She could get lost in him, and for a brief moment, she couldn't remember if she was in India or D.C. Then she reluctantly reminded herself that this is what he did, that the best players knew how to be at least a little genuine.

She cleared her throat, trying to get herself refocused on the task at hand. "There are so many amazing photographers, I don't know how we'll choose which images to use."

Chase's gaze lingered on her, then he took a swig of his beer. "I was thinking we should aim for a mix of beautiful animals and landscapes and some of the more alarming images that show the effects of climate change," he said. "That way we can create a sense of urgency without making everyone feel totally hopeless."

She was impressed again by his insightfulness. "I think that's the perfect approach. Mixing paintings and photographs would help balance the mood, too."

He nodded and cleared his throat. "We should probably get back to it," he said.

They went inside, and Rayne dumped the plates in the sink then joined Chase in the living room. He'd resumed his position on the floor.

"I saved my portfolio for last," he said.

When she saw his photos, Rayne said a soft "Wow!" that made him smile. "These are gorgeous."

Then she was pointing and asking "Where's this?" and "How did you get this shot?" and "When was this taken?" Among the photos, she recognized a place her parents had taken her—Brindavan Gardens in India. "I've been there! I remember those mango and avocado trees, and the allamanda in bloom. I loved those pretty yellow flowers. They have a sort of light fruity smell. I kept sticking my nose in them. You've really captured it. Well, except for the smell."

He laughed. "I haven't figured out how to capture smells in photography. Which is probably just as well. I'm assuming your parents took you to Agra to see the Taj Mahal?"

She nodded. "What tourist could resist?"

"Then I'm sure you remember the smell of garbage and sewage."

She wrinkled her nose. "How could I forget!"

He finished his beer and took her empty bottle from her hand and headed to the kitchen. "So when's the last time you were overseas?" he asked as he popped open the last two beers.

She leaned her head back against the couch as she thought about it, feeling full and sleepy and relaxed. He came back with the beers and handed her one. His gaze strayed to her throat, and the look in his eyes sent a wave of heat through her body.

"It's been years," she said. "I haven't even gone beyond Maryland since I came to D.C. for college and then work."

"Where are your parents now?" he asked as he sat down beside her.

"Vermont. They got a little farm there a couple years ago. It's about the longest they've stayed anywhere."

He took a swig of his beer. "So you haven't seen your parents in a couple years?"

"They've come down here to visit me once or twice, but I haven't made it up that way yet. I'm sure I will eventually."

She was aware of him watching her, aware of the heat of his body next to hers. Aware that he only needed to lean forward a little if wanted to kiss her. Aware, too, that she was supposed to be avoiding such thoughts, but she couldn't muster the energy to resist them.

"All that moving around must have been tough on you as a kid," he said.

"Yeah, it wasn't great." She picked at the label on the beer bottle. "They wanted to live off the grid. They were all about self-sufficiency. Even communes were too structured for them, so we moved to communities—and I use that term loosely—that were tolerant of people who didn't want traditional lifestyles."

She stretched out her legs, brushing against his thigh in the process. It wasn't entirely accidental, and he didn't move away. "I didn't mind going to the schools in those areas because all the kids were in the same boat. But in other places, I was the only kid in town wearing handmade clothes, who brought hummus and bean sprout sandwiches on homemade bread for lunch. I used to bribe the other kids for potato chips and Twinkies when I could."

He smiled. "Somehow I can't picture you eating chips and Twinkies."

"Hey, we all have our vices," she said with a smile. "I kept wanting my parents to pick one of those places to stay—I didn't even care which one. But we always seemed to move right when I was getting settled."

She took a long drink of her beer. "It would have been nice not to feel like an outsider all the time."

He was silent for a moment. "It certainly gives you a different perspective—being the stranger in town," he said. "It works for me as a photographer."

She looked over at him. "People are drawn to you because you're different?"

"It has a way of making me the center of attention—for good and bad."

"But eventually, you have to get to know people to get access to places, right?"

"I hadn't thought of it that way, but sure. I need to be good at chatting people up, finding out what's important to them."

She smiled. "Is that what you're doing now?"

He turned to look at her. She had such an urge to touch his handsome, rugged face with her fingertips, to put her mouth on those kissable lips. He was gazing at her openly with his beautiful blue eyes, and he started to say something then stopped himself.

"Just making friendly conversation," he finally said. "So you haven't ventured out of D.C. in what—six or seven years?"

"More like eight," she said.

He finished off his beer. "I can't imagine staying put that long."

"But you are staying put in a way," she said. "You keep coming back to D.C."

"Not the same thing. This is just a landing spot. I feel like my real life is out there." He waved an arm toward the window.

"On the front porch?" she teased.

He laughed. "I'd be willing to venture onto the sidewalk under the right conditions."

"I think your life is there," she said softly. "And here."

He turned to look at her again, and she saw the desire in his eyes and knew he wanted to kiss her. And as much as she wanted him to, she was relieved when he didn't.

"I should get going," he said, his voice suddenly rough. "I want to start hitting up some photographers for images to donate, and I'm sure you've got other things to do."

He shut down his laptop and gathered up his notes. "How's your neighbor doing, by the way?"

Rayne was surprised and pleased that he remembered. "She's doing much better, thanks for asking."

He slid his laptop into his bag, and she walked with him to the door.

"I can't thank you enough for helping with this," she said.

"My pleasure. Plus, it gives me something to do while I'm waiting on my next gig."

"Hey, whatever happened with that guy we saw at Zipped? Did you find out about the assignment in Nepal?"

"Still working on it," he said.

She felt a stab of disappointment that he was trying to go away. But that was who he was and other women had doubtless tried to get him to stay, which made her think of Crystal. She suddenly felt like crap for even thinking about kissing him.

He was halfway down the porch steps when he turned and said, "My mother has a killer Christmas card list. I'm going to see if she'll give me a copy—or maybe even send everyone a personal note about the event."

Rayne smiled. "I want to meet this woman!"

"She'd like you." Then he turned—a little abruptly, Rayne thought—and walked away.

She watched him go, thinking Crystal wouldn't mind if she took a moment to enjoy the way his long legs and firm ass rocked those Levis.

Chapter 6

After he left Rayne's house, Chase headed for Sweet Happens, thinking a hazelnut coffee would be just the thing to clear his head. He'd had such high hopes for the afternoon. Rayne had started out a little distant and jumped away the first time she brushed against him, but then by the end, she had sidled closer and was relaxed and cozy and so damn kissable. She had that sleepy, flushed look that made him lose his mind. He imagined that's how she'd look in bed, after he'd—

"Focus, man!" he said out loud.

He needed to figure this thing out because it was starting to drive him crazy that he couldn't just touch her, couldn't just kiss her. As soon as he thought he might have a chance with her, she seemed to withdraw and Colin's warning rang in his ears. And he was starting to worry that the longer he waited, the harder it would be to walk away.

As Sweet Happens came into view, he realized he shouldn't go in. He didn't want to give Crystal the wrong idea. She'd already texted him a couple times since they'd gone to the opening together on Thursday, and he'd been friendly but not overly so. Still, he knew it was just a matter of time before she came up with a reason for him to come over to her place. He'd had fun with her at the event, and there was no denying how hot she was, but he didn't like her the way she obviously liked him. If she could have kept it casual maybe—but at the notion of a meaningless fling with Crystal, he immediately thought of Rayne and felt guilty.

As he veered away from Sweet Happens, he couldn't remember ever having so much trouble navigating between women. He took it as a sign that he'd been in town too long.

Life in D.C. got damn complicated when he stayed put.

Sweet Happens was out, but he didn't feel like going go back to his empty apartment so he decided to walk over to Zipped.

There were a few groups of people eating dinner when Chase got there. He sat down at the bar, and Colin walked over a few minutes later with a glass of water and a cup of coffee.

Chase shook his head in amazement. "I don't know how you do that, man, but you're always dead-on. How'd you know I didn't want a beer—or something stronger?"

Colin shrugged. "Elementary, my dear Watson," he said with a terrible English accent that made Chase cringe. Ever since Colin had fallen in love with Savannah, he was so cheerful and, well, goofy.

"You're a little bleary-eyed," Colin continued, "your shoulders are slumped, and you're moving slow. So you've obviously already had a beer, or two."

"Damn, you're good."

"Been watching Swamp People all day?" Colin asked as he fixed a gin and tonic for a customer.

Chase took a sip of his coffee and felt his head begin to clear. He thought about lying, but Rayne would tell Savannah and Savannah would tell Colin.

"No, I was helping Rayne with her fundraising thing," he said.

Colin set the drink on a tray with a few others and held it out as Diana swung by. She picked it up in one fluid motion.

"Hey, Chase," she said as she passed him.

"Hey, babe."

"I hear that fundraiser was your idea," Colin said to Chase.

"We sort of came up with it together. I just encouraged her to do it."

Colin braced his hands on the bar and pinned Chase with a serious look. "Savannah said you were over there the other night, too. She's pretty concerned that you're not taking us seriously about steering clear of Rayne."

"I don't see how it's any of Savannah's business."

Colin gave him a look that didn't need words.

"OK, OK, I get it," Chase said, putting his hands up in surrender. "They're chick bonded, BFFs and all that. But seriously, Rayne is a grown woman. You guys talk about her as though she's some fragile girl who needs babysitting."

Diana came up beside Chase. "Who's fragile?" she asked. "And do you want wings or a burger?"

"Burger," Chase said. "And we were talking about Rayne."

"That adorable girl who tips a ten every time?" Diana asked. "I like her. I say go for it."

Chase grinned.

"Thanks, D. You're a big help," Colin said as he picked up a towel and started wiping down glasses behind the bar.

Diana shrugged. "I just call it as I see it. I think she's a keeper. I'm also pretty sure that she's past the age of consent and can make up her own mind," she said with a pointed look at Colin. Turning to Chase, she asked, "French fries or onion rings?"

"Fries," Chase said. "You need to learn to do that thing Colin does with drinks so we can skip all this ordering business."

"Unlike Colin, I like to let people make their own decisions."

"Truly a wise woman," Chase said as Diana walked away.

Colin sighed. "Do what you want, but if you're dating Crystal and you start messing around with Rayne and hurt her, Savannah's going to be upset, and if Savannah's upset—"

Chase interrupted him. "Who said I was dating Crystal?"

"Savannah did."

"Where the hell did she get that idea?"

"She said Rayne told her."

"What the hell?" Chase suddenly remembered the Sweet Happens box on Rayne's counter the other day, and then she'd asked him that afternoon whether he'd seen Crystal at the opening. If she'd known he was lying, why hadn't she called him on it? But if she thought Chase was dating Crystal, then her behavior was starting to make more sense.

"What can I tell you, bro," Colin said, interrupting Chase's line of thought. "There's this whole chick communication network we're not even aware of. I think it's in the cloud or something."

Chase leaned forward. "First of all, I'm not dating Crystal. She invited me to Roger Thaw's opening, and it was a golden opportunity for me to do some networking."

"And she's hot and you've got a history."

"No, man. Seriously. It wasn't like that. We had a nice time, but nothing happened."

Colin picked up some empty glasses and dumped them into a rubber bin behind the counter. "Just let me know before you leave town again so I can start going somewhere else for my coffee. Crystal was seriously upset when you took off the last time."

"I'm not hooking up with—"

Colin cut him off. "I'm just saying that actions have consequences. Even if you aren't here to see them."

Colin moved off down the bar before Chase could respond. His head was spinning, and for once in his life, he wasn't sure what he wanted. No, strike that—he knew what he wanted, but he didn't know how to go about getting it. He wanted Rayne. He wanted to slowly, ever so slowly peel away all her clothes and explore every inch of her body and watch her smoky gray eyes smolder. He wanted to lick that sweet perfume she'd been wearing right off her skin. He wanted to stroke and caress and nibble until he knew every spot that gave her pleasure. He wanted to be the reason for her tousled hair and flushed cheeks.

But he didn't know how to do that without getting tangled up and ultimately hurting her. It was never really easy to walk away from relationships. That's why he always seemed to find a reason to leave town when the time was right, and the woman's anger did the rest. But he didn't like the idea of doing that to Rayne, and it hamstrung him in a way he'd never experienced.

Diana brought him his burger and fries and offered to refill his coffee. "No, thanks," he said. His brain already hurt, and he had a feeling he was going to have a hard enough time sleeping as it was.

He took a bite of the burger, but he wasn't all that hungry either. He was remembering the sandwich Rayne had made for him and how good it had tasted—and how good it felt to have someone like her taking care of him. And now he felt miserable.

Colin came by and helped himself to some of Chase's fries.

"Why is Savannah so damn protective of Rayne?" Chase asked. "If I'm such a scoundrel, why can't she be trusted to tell me to get lost on her own?"

"I don't know," Colin said. "Savannah just said Rayne had some history, some guy really did a number on her a year or so ago, and Savannah sees something in you that's bringing it all back."

"Damn those guys," Chase said.

Colin gave him a pointed look. "You have been that guy for plenty of women."

Chase knew he was right. "I must be losing my touch. I used to be able to pick out the women who were on the same wavelength. Have some fun, have some sex, move on. But lately—"

"Life getting a little too real for you, bro?"

Chase looked up at him. "Something like that."

"About time for you to take off for Timbuktu, isn't it?"

"Thanks for reminding me!" Chase pulled his phone out of his pocket to check his email and was excited to see that Ben had finally sent him a note about the gig in Nepal. He said the magazine looked legit and included the email address of the guy in charge so Chase could contact him directly. Chase immediately sent the guy a message saying he'd heard about the potential assignment in Nepal and had experience in that part of the world. He included a link to his online portfolio, which also had some client testimonials, and said he could leave at a moment's notice.

Chase glanced up as Colin came around from behind the bar, his face suddenly lit up with a big smile. Chase turned around in his chair and saw that Savannah had walked in.

"Hey, sweetie," Colin said as he put his arms around her and held her close, planting a kiss on the curve of her neck. "Did you get your work done?"

Savannah gave him a quick kiss on the mouth before answering. "Yeah, I think I'm all caught up."

Letting go of Colin, she walked over to the bar and hopped up on the stool next to Chase.

"Hungry?" Colin asked as he walked back around the bar.

"Starving." She eyed the fries on Chase's plate.

"I recommend the burger and fries," Chase said. He wiped his mouth with a napkin and grabbed his laptop bag, sliding the plate toward Savannah. "I'll leave you two lovebirds alone. But try to keep it down tonight. Some of us need our beauty sleep."

"Hey, I make no promises," Colin said. And the loving gaze he turned on a grinning Savannah made Chase feel a flash of something unfamiliar—was it envy?

Christ, he needed to get to Timbuktu.

By the time he got home that night, Chase had resolved to keep his distance from Rayne and focus on getting the gig in Nepal or anything else that would take him out of town and away from all romantic entanglements.

For the next week, he kept himself busy and tried to steer clear of seeing Rayne, though he couldn't avoid communicating with her about the gala. But that felt safe; he could handle that. He spent some time composing an email message to the list of artists and photographers the two of them had come up with, and then he sent her the text to review, with a note saying he'd enjoyed hanging out with her. It seemed like the natural thing to do.

When she emailed back her revisions, she said she'd enjoyed herself, too.

He sent the message out to the artists, asking them to respond in ten days. He figured he'd follow up with phone calls to most of them, partly for his own personal networking and partly because he wanted Rayne's event to be a success. And because he was only human, he allowed himself a moment to imagine her in a skimpy cocktail dress and the look of gratitude she'd give him, laced with desire.

Later in the week, he culled through the photos he'd taken at his parents' house and put the best ones up on a private page of his website and emailed a link to his mother so she could pick out her favorites. But he knew she didn't check email every day so he called to tell her what he'd done.

"Let me know which ones you like and whether you want me to handle getting the prints," he said.

"Thank you, sweetheart. I'll take a look just as soon as I get a chance."

"And hey, I was wondering if you'd part with your Christmas mailing list. It's for a good cause."

"Of course," she said. "What's the cause?"

"I'm helping a friend put on a fundraiser, for the Center for Action on Climate Change. We're going to have a fancy gala and auction off a bunch of photos and other artwork. You should put it on your calendar."

He gave her the date and heard her flipping through her desk planner. "Yes, I can be there. I'll have to check with your father. And I'll email you a copy of the mailing list."

"I think it would be even better if the note came from you," Chase said. "They're making up some invitations, but maybe you could write a little something...?"

"I'd be happy to. It's so nice to see you involved with a philanthropic venture," she said, and he could tell she was smiling. "Is this 'friend' the girl who lost her phone?"

"Woman, Mom. And yes, it's for Rayne."

"Rayne. That's an unusual name. Where have I heard that before?"

"She's Savannah's roommate. You didn't meet her, but she was at the wine bar back in June when Colin gave Dad his sales pitch."

"Ah yes. She was having a drink with you and Jessica at the bar. I'm sorry I didn't get a chance to talk to her."

"She's dying to meet you, too. I should set you two up on a date."

"I'd enjoy that, and you should come, too. Pick any of our restaurants and name the time, and your father and I will meet you there."

"Whoa, Mom!" Chase said with a laugh. "I was teasing. We're just friends. And even if we were more, it would be years before

I'd be ready to subject her to dinner with Dad at one of his restaurants."

His mother laughed, too. "Fair enough. I'll look through your photos this week and let you know."

"Great. And thanks for helping out with the gala."

"Anything for you, dear. And your *friend*."

She emphasized the word "friend" in a way that let him know she was hoping for more. So far she was the only person—himself included—who hadn't told him to back off.

He hung up and then held onto his phone for a moment, thinking he'd like to call Rayne. His little fantasy of her in a cocktail dress was undermining his resolve to keep his distance, though, so he decided to text her instead.

Good news! My mom will personally send invites to her whole list.

When Rayne replied almost immediately, he was irrationally pleased, as though maybe she'd been keeping an eye on her phone and hoping to hear from him.

"Get a grip, man!" he muttered as he opened her message, which said: *Wow! That's great news!!*

He grinned at her enthusiastic response and tried to think of a way to keep the conversation going when another message popped up.

Could we look at the list first to make sure it doesn't overlap with ours?

His smile faded at her business-like tone, and he shook his head. He really did need to get a grip. He couldn't remember ever letting a woman reduce him to the emotional equivalent of a teenager, not even when he actually was a teenager.

He typed back, *Good thinking. I'll email it ASAP.*

Rayne's response was a smiley face emoji, and he stared at his phone for several long moments, but the conversation was over.

As he headed for the kitchen to grab a beer, even though it was the middle of the afternoon, he congratulated himself on being a stand-up guy: He was helping Rayne and helping the environment, and he wasn't doing it to get Rayne into bed. As he popped open the beer and flicked on the TV, he ignored the part of his brain that said if he truly was a stand-up guy, he'd be able to make a phone call without worrying about going off the rails.

Chapter 7

A few days later, Chase had started to seriously hate having a conscience. He was itching to see Rayne. He'd been having an ongoing email discussion with Ben's contact about the gig in Nepal, but the guy was being a little cagey, and Chase was thinking about just getting on a plane to anywhere so he could feel normal again.

Then a text message popped up from Rayne: *Invitations will be ready Thursday. I can courier some to your mom. Just need the address.*

He didn't even hesitate before texting back: *I can swing by that day and pick them up.* He still had the business card his mom had given him, so he already knew her work address.

Are you sure? I don't want to put you out.

No problem. Around 4:00?

He was thinking that they'd chat a little and then go for a drink. After a glass of wine, maybe she'd open up about the guy from her past who had her so spooked. For one brief moment when he was sitting on her living room floor, he'd seen the desire in her eyes. She wanted him, he was sure of it. He just had to figure out a way to make it work without hurting her.

After a pause that felt longer then the two minutes it actually was, Rayne texted back: *4 is good. See ya then!*

As soon as he turned the corner and saw the house where Rayne worked, Chase understood why she felt so passionate about saving it. Despite being crowded on all sides by new buildings, it still managed to look dignified without being showy. A brick pathway led to a low porch with widely spaced columns and a double door flanked by floor-to-ceiling windows with dark green shutters. There was a full-length bay window above the front door and brick chimneys jutting out of either end of the roof. The house had a pleasing symmetry and a quiet elegance.

He took out his cell phone and snapped a few photos then crossed the porch to the front door. He paused in the foyer, and a woman in a knee-length navy blue skirt and white silk blouse came out of the room to his left. Her blond hair was swept back from her face by a wide velvet hair band. Chase couldn't help admiring the way her snug skirt and blousy top accented her curves in all the right ways.

"Can I help you?" she asked.

"I'm here to see Rayne Michael."

"You must be Chase Allison," she said. "She told me you'd be stopping by. I'm Sheila. We're so grateful for your help. You are truly a lifesaver."

He smiled and waved away the compliment. "Rayne's doing all the real work. I'm just getting some pictures together."

"Don't be so modest. Your connections are going to be the difference between a good event and a hugely successful one." Her blue eyes twinkled, and he had a flash of the clichéd sexy librarian, minus the glasses.

"I don't know about that." Unless he was totally off his game, she was flirting with him. If it wasn't for Rayne, he'd probably be asking Sheila out for a drink already.

"Trust me, we couldn't do it without your artistic expertise," she said with a warm smile. "I'll let Rayne know you're here."

He expected her to lead him upstairs because Rayne had said something about her office being a former bedroom, which had conjured all sorts of fantasies in his mind. But instead, Sheila led him back into her office and then opened the door to the next room.

Chase stepped inside. Rayne was on the far side of a huge oak desk that was strewn with papers. The sight of her made his heart give a little jump—until he saw the man she was standing next to. Chase felt a hot pang of jealousy. He should have stuck to texting.

Rayne looked up at him, her face blank for a moment. Then she smiled. "Is it 4:00 already? I totally lost track of time."

Chase smiled back, but he noticed that she still hadn't moved away from the man.

"You must be Chase Allison," the man said. He came over to shake Chase's hand. "I'm Jeremy Banks. It's a pleasure to finally meet you. I can't thank you enough for your help."

The man looked like he'd stepped from the pages of a magazine, he was that kind of good-looking. Smooth and intelligent, too. And he surrounded himself with smart, beautiful women. Chase felt a grudging admiration, but mostly he felt outclassed and awkward as hell.

"Happy to help," Chase said.

"And your mother has been generous, too," Jeremy said. "I'd like to send her a token of our thanks. Flowers maybe?"

Chase had an image of this man going toe to toe with his father and honestly didn't know who would win. Maybe flowers from a handsome stranger would make his father appreciate her more.

"She'd love that," he said. He took a business card from his wallet and jotted down his parents' address and handed it to Jeremy.

"I'll get you those invitations," Rayne said. "They're in my office."

"Nice meeting you," Chase said to Jeremy, who nodded and smiled. Then Chase followed Rayne out into the foyer.

"So that's your boss?" he said as they walked up the stairs.

"Yeah. He's amazing," Rayne said with more enthusiasm than Chase would have liked. "And best of all, he's convinced the landlord to sell us the building! Jeremy really can work miracles. We just have to figure out how to get Vincent to come down on the asking price."

"That's great news," Chase said, trying to shrug off the jealousy he was feeling and hoping she didn't pick up on it. "Oh, hey, now that I've seen this place, I was thinking we should have a photo or two of the house at the gala. I could bring my equipment one day and take some shots."

She turned to him with a look of pleasure on her face. "You're a genius!" she said, grabbing his arm in her excitement.

"I can't believe I didn't think of that before! Maybe we could even sell some smaller prints at the event—and we could use the photo in the promotional materials."

Chase glanced down at her hand on his arm, and she instantly let go. But when he looked up into her smoky gray eyes, he knew she'd felt the same jolt of electricity he had. She gave him a little half-smile and nervously smoothed her hair behind her ear then started walking again.

He couldn't help appreciating the way her short black skirt hugged her ass and showed off her legs as she led him up the stairs and into a room that was flooded with late-afternoon sunlight from a set of windows on the far side. Her desk was smaller but looked about as old as the one in Jeremy's office, and it, too, was covered with papers. His eye was drawn to the vintage-looking loveseat in the corner, a perfect spot for canoodling.

"Here are the invitations and the envelopes," she said, breaking into his reverie. She handed him two boxes and a manila folder. "We printed out the labels from your mother's list after we cross-checked them with our own. There was some overlap, but we figured we'd let her contact those people. That personal touch really makes a difference."

He put the stuff in his shoulder bag. "I'll take these to her tomorrow and maybe stick around and help her address a few."

"I'm sure she'll appreciate that." Rayne turned back to her desk. "Oh, and just drop them in any mailbox—we already put stamps on all the envelopes."

"Great, and, uh, by the way," he said, trying to regain her full attention. "I've gotten a bunch of responses to the email I sent out to the photographers and artists. I thought we could go over the submissions together. Maybe this weekend?"

She was looking through a stack of papers on her desk, trying to find something. "This weekend?"

He had been hoping for more enthusiasm. "Are you busy?"

"No more than usual," she said, triumphantly pulling out a manila folder.

"What if I come by your place on Saturday?" he asked.

She looked up at him as if suddenly clueing into what they were talking about. After a pause, she said, "Evening would be best. Around 6:00?"

"That works," he said with a smile. He was about to ask her to go for a drink when Sheila popped her head in the doorway.

"Jeremy wants to know whether you want Indian or Vietnamese," Sheila said to Rayne.

"Hmmmm... Vietnamese."

Sheila nodded and disappeared.

"You guys are having dinner together?" Chase asked, hoping his voice didn't sound as strange to her as it did to him.

"Ordering in because we're working late," she said. "I knew there would be a ton of work for this thing, but I had no idea how much."

She walked out of the office, and he followed her down the stairs.

"I bet his wife isn't crazy about him working late," Chase said, trying to sound casual.

"Jeremy's not married," Rayne said.

Of course he's not, Chase thought, and wasn't sure how to interpret the smile that lingered on her face.

At the door, she put her hand on his arm and said, "Thanks again for stopping by. I'll see you Saturday." Then she headed into Jeremy's office.

Out on the sidewalk, Chase resisted the urge to look back at the house and see whether he could catch a glimpse of Rayne through the large downstairs window. With Jeremy. He was getting that restless feeling again, so he decided to walk home.

A few blocks later, he saw Sweet Happens and swung inside for a little pick-me-up. He was surprised to find the place empty of customers.

Crystal's face lit up when she saw him. "Hey, you," she said. "Hazelnut coffee time?"

"Hey." He walked up to the counter and eyed the pastries in the display case. "I'm thinking about changing things up a little. How about a scone? And maybe some tea?"

"Earl Grey?"

"Great! Put it in a to-go cup. I'll take it with me."

"Sure thing."

She got his tea and put the scone in a white paper bag. He pulled money out of his wallet and set it on the counter before she could protest. "Keep the change," he said and started for the door.

"So, hey, Rayne asked me to donate one of my paintings for the fundraiser she's putting together," Crystal said. He turned back around, and she was beaming.

"That's fantastic," Chase said. "You guys must be pretty good friends." He was thinking about Rayne's standoffishness and thinking that if he was the stand-up guy he wished he was, he'd set Crystal straight sometime soon, for everyone's sake.

"She and Savannah come in here a lot," Crystal said. "And Rayne asked about my paintings as soon as I put them up. She must have really liked them."

"You do good work," Chase said, and he meant it.

"I'm so excited. I'd love your help picking the right one. Maybe you could come by some night after I close and go through them with me?"

He paused. The hot tea was searing his hand through the paper cup, and he was wishing like hell he'd stopped at a Starbucks instead, preferably one in Timbuktu.

"Why don't you email me some images and I'll take a look," he said.

"Well, I've got some new cupcake flavors I wanted to try out and this bottle of ice wine I picked up at a tasting awhile back, so I thought maybe we could make an evening of it." Crystal kept her gaze averted and brushed invisible crumbs off the top of the display case as she spoke.

He'd known this was coming. Man, he hated these conversations. "Ah, Crystal. I don't think that's a good idea."

"Why? Do you suddenly prefer red wine?" she said, finally lifting her gaze to him. From the look on her face, she already guessed what he was going to say.

"I like hanging out with you, Crystal, I really do. It's just—"

She'd gone very still and quiet, but he could feel the anger and hurt starting to radiate from her. "Just what?" she said.

"I mean, we've tried this before, and it didn't work out so well. You know how I am. I never stick around for long, and you deserve someone who will be here all the time."

"I'm a big girl," she said, hurt flashing in her eyes. "I can decide for myself what I do or do not deserve. And I know exactly who you are, Chase Allison."

He'd forgotten how quickly she could switch from sweet to fired up. And once she got going, it was hard to turn it off.

"Don't try to make out like you're doing me a favor," she continued, her voice getting louder with every word. "Like you're some kind of hero. If you're not attracted to me anymore, just say so."

"It's not that." Oh, god, why had he said that? "I mean, you're beautiful and sexy, and I honestly enjoy spending time with you." He was only getting himself in deeper. He wished he could hit the "undo" button.

Her expression softened slightly, and she put her hands on her hips. "So what's the problem?"

"The problem is—" Chase stopped, suddenly aware that he couldn't answer honestly without revealing his feelings about Rayne. And even though he didn't know exactly what those feelings were, he was pretty sure Crystal wasn't the first person he should be telling.

"The problem is, ah…that… I'm trying to change, to be better about how I treat women." It sounded lame, but it wasn't entirely insincere. "I shouldn't have gone with you to Thaw's opening. I didn't want to lead you on, and I thought we could be friends. You said that's what you wanted, too."

"I lied, OK?" She'd flipped back to anger now, and Chase was starting to get a headache.

"I'm sorry, Crystal, I really am."

She glared at him, and the longer she stared, the more uncomfortable he got. He was thinking about leaving before he could cause any more trouble when her eyes suddenly got wide.

"You're sleeping with someone else," she said.

"What? No."

"Of course you are. I'm such an idiot! You've been in town for months now, and you always make sure you've got something going with someone. I guess I should be glad that you're a one-woman man in your own small way."

She turned away to go into the kitchen.

"I hate leaving things like this," he called after her. "Why don't I come over and look at your paintings tomorrow night?"

"Forget it," she said over her shoulder. "I don't need your pity."

"What can I do?"

"For starters, you can get out of my shop."

He decided to leave before she came up with a whole list of things for him to do that likely ended with a one-way trip to hell.

Chapter 8

Rayne had been spending so much time with Jeremy that they had fallen into a comfortable sort of closeness, the kind where they could anticipate what the other person was thinking—about work at least. She was under no illusions about what it meant, but she was enjoying herself just the same.

And then Chase had walked in looking rugged and handsome, and it was so strange to see him in Jeremy's office. She had lost track of time, her head was full of details about the event, and she couldn't process the sight of him or the sensation it triggered, a pleasant sort of electricity that buzzed through her whole body.

So now she was baffled that she'd told him to come by at 6:00 on Saturday. It meant she'd have to make him dinner, which was way different from fixing some sandwiches, and it meant they'd be alone at the house. Carol was out of town all weekend, and Savannah had already told Rayne she'd be with Colin on Saturday night. Rayne would not have suggested it if she'd been thinking clearly. But she never seemed to be thinking clearly when Chase was involved.

She kept telling herself it wasn't a date—he was with Crystal—and she had to keep things casual. On Saturday afternoon, she walked over to Eastern Market, where she went almost every weekend in the summer because she loved strolling through the historic main building with its food stalls and then wandering among the kiosks outside and browsing the funky clothes and jewelry.

As she wandered through the crowded market comparing the quality and prices of the various vegetable sellers, she paused to listen to a band playing in the parking lot near the school. A woman was belting out "Me and Bobby McGee" in a voice eerily similar to Janice Joplin's, and it gave her a chill.

She ended up buying fresh salad greens, heirloom tomatoes, bell peppers, a block of havarti cheese, free-range eggs, and fresh-baked rolls. Later, she walked over to Sweet Happens to find something suitably casual for dessert. The heat of summer was retreating, and it was pleasantly warm and breezy. The door to the cafe was propped open to take advantage of the weather, but Crystal wasn't her usual perky self when Rayne walked in. In fact, she looked like she'd been crying.

"Everything OK?" Rayne asked.

"Yeah, fine," Crystal said, but her voice was flat. Then she made an effort to smile. "Sorry—you caught me in a fit of self-pity."

"I'm sorry to hear that. Nothing serious, I hope...?"

"Just a serious case of me being an idiot." Crystal shook her head. "I always seem to waste my time on the wrong guys."

"Tell me about it!" Rayne said. Then it dawned on her. "Are you talking about Chase?"

"Yeah." Crystal sighed. "We went to that photography opening I told you about, and we had a great time. But he's been evasive ever since, and then the other day he tells me he's sleeping with someone else."

Rayne felt a flush of heat and a wave of nausea that she knew was jealousy. She also knew she had no reason to feel it, but that didn't make it go away.

"I'm so sorry, Crystal!" she said. "I didn't know he was like that."

"He's definitely some kind of player, but he usually sticks to just one woman at a time. See, that's the thing—I know he's into me, but he's been distracted for the last month or so, and now I know why. He loves the chase." She stared at Rayne, who was still lost in thought. "That was a joke, a play on words: Chase loves the chase."

Rayne smiled. "I get it. And I'm glad you can laugh about it. Who needs him, right? If he doesn't know a great woman when he sees one, it's his loss."

"Yeah, you're right. He's the poster child for commitment

phobia. But in his defense, much as I hate to admit it, he never led me to expect anything else from him. If I could have kept things casual, like he does, everything would have been cool." She sighed. "But I just can't do casual, not once sex is involved."

"I know what you mean," Rayne said.

"But hey, you didn't come in here to talk about Chase. What can I get you?"

Rayne was suddenly uncomfortable. In a way, she had come in to talk about Chase, or at least to buy dessert for him.

"Do you have any of those little fruit tarts?" she asked.

"No, sorry, I'm all out. I made some cream puffs today though."

"That sounds good. I'll take half a dozen."

"They're in the refrigerator in the back. You and Savannah hanging out tonight? Want me to throw in some cupcakes?"

"Savannah's with Colin tonight. I...uh... I've got a friend coming over to help me with the fundraiser."

What was it about Chase that had her lying all over town? She hadn't told Savannah that he was coming over because Savannah hadn't asked what Rayne was up to. But it was a sin of omission. Now she was doing the same thing to Crystal. She told herself she was doing it to keep from looking like an idiot after everything Crystal had just said about him.

But the truth was, he felt like a secret she was keeping even from herself.

When Rayne got home, she changed into a denim skirt that flared around her knees and a short-sleeved linen blouse. Then she put together a simple quiche and tossed the leftover vegetables in with the salad greens. She was straightening up the living room when Chase showed up a few minutes before 6:00 with a bottle of Chardonnay. He was wearing jeans and a lightweight knit shirt in navy blue with the long sleeves pushed up over his muscular forearms. The shirt was snug over his equally muscular chest, and he smelled of a woodsy, musky soap-and-aftershave combo. She liked the scent—a lot.

Chase followed her into the kitchen. "Something smells

amazing." She smiled to herself. At least they were sort of on the same wavelength.

"Don't get too excited, it's just a basic quiche," Rayne said as the timer sounded and she reached for her rooster pot holders.

"You know how much I like anything that's home cooked," he said.

Rayne bent over to take the quiche out of the oven, and when she turned, she noticed that Chase's gaze had to work its way up from her ass to her eyes. She felt a little thrill, and it made her smile.

"So where's Savannah tonight?" he asked as he leaned against the counter.

"She's hanging out with Colin at the wine bar. He was having dinner with her, then she was going to go to his place—your place—and wait for him to get done with work."

She handed Chase a corkscrew, and he starting peeling the foil from the wine bottle while she dug some glasses out of the cabinet. It occurred to her that they hadn't discussed eating—or drinking—this evening. They had both just assumed. She liked the feeling of being in sync with someone, with him specifically.

"You have another roommate, right? Karen?" he asked.

Rayne laughed. Chase was notoriously bad with names. "Carol. She's off at a work conference for the next few days."

He removed the cork with a pop. "So you mean you and I are without adult supervision?"

"Looks that way," Rayne said and then without thinking added, "Should I have gotten a chaperone?"

He looked startled, but then he grinned. "I'm not sure how to answer that."

She blushed in embarrassment. "Just kidding," she said and turned away to get the salad out of the fridge. She took advantage of the opportunity to remind herself that he was sleeping with someone and this was not a date—no matter how much it felt like one. No matter how much she wished it were one.

She scooped the salad into two bowls, slid two slices of quiche onto plates, and handed one of each to Chase, who followed her into the living room where she'd already set the bread and cheese. Chase ran back to the kitchen for the wine, and they made themselves comfortable on the floor with the laptop on the table in front of them.

They ate and drank wine as they looked at images of what the artists were donating to the auction. Rayne took notes on sizes and prices and kept a running tally of the amounts to see if they would hit their goal. They could do it but only if all the images sold for the high end of where the artists had priced them. She tapped her pencil on the notepad, lost in thought. Then she was suddenly aware that she hadn't spoken in several moments and glanced over to see Chase sipping his wine and watching her.

"Something wrong?" he asked.

"We're so close," she said. "If we could just negotiate a lower price with Vincent, we would hit the mark no problem."

He took the pencil from her and did some math of his own. "I think Thaw's photos could go for quite a bit more, so we should just raise the minimum on those. And I'll throw in a couple more of my own, and if we bump up a few of these prices—"

Rayne peered over his shoulder. "This could actually work!" she said, and a feeling of relief and excitement washed over her.

"You sound surprised," Chase said, setting down the notepad and picking up his wine glass.

"I was never really sure. I mean, no offense to you, but there are so many variables. You have done an incredible job of pulling all these artists together."

He shrugged, but he was smiling. "Networking is what I do."

She got to her feet, a little awkwardly because she was feeling the effects of the wine despite their dinner. Chase stood up, too, and helped her carry the dishes to the kitchen then refilled their wine glasses and held onto the bottle. As she followed him back into the living room, she couldn't help thinking how much she was enjoying the evening, how comfortable and easy she felt with him, and how good his ass looked in those well-worn jeans.

Chase put the wine bottle on the table, but this time, he sat on the couch instead of the floor. She sat down beside him and sank into the cushions, tucking her feet under her and turning slightly to face him. She'd been running herself a little ragged, and now she was feeling a pleasant, relaxed sort of fatigue.

Chase said, "So how was your dinner with Jeremy the other night?"

"Hmmm?" she asked, resisting a strong urge to lean in and smell him again, maybe rest her head on his shoulder the way she had that night months ago at Zipped when she'd had enough gin and tonics to be as relaxed as she was now. She was a little surprised that Chase had never mentioned that night, but she'd figured it hadn't been that memorable to him.

"Rayne?" Chase said, and she realized she'd been staring at him a little dreamily instead of answering his question.

"Oh! Um, it was fine." She shook her head a little to try to clear it. "We got a lot of work done. And he ordered flowers for your mom."

"Nice guy," Chase said, taking another sip of wine.

"Yeah, he's pretty dreamy."

Chase laughed. "Has anyone used that word since the 1950s?"

She blushed and laughed with him. "Sorry. He's handsome and he's my boss and that's that."

"Oh? Never had the urge to pursue him?"

"Nope." The sun had gone down and the only light in the room came from the moon and the streetlight outside. She swirled the wine in the glass and watched it shimmer. "I've learned my lesson."

"What lesson is that?" he asked, shifting his body toward her and draping his arm across the back of the couch. She looked away, keeping her eyes on her wine glass as she thought about the simplest way to explain her disastrous relationship with Brandon.

"I don't get involved with men I work with," she finally said.

"Does that include me?"

She slowly raised her eyes to his, expecting to see him grinning and teasing, but his serious expression confused her. Every cell in her body told her the attraction between them was mutual and real. But then she remembered her conversation with Crystal and didn't know how to answer his question—she wasn't even sure she'd understood him right.

"I saw Crystal today," she said, figuring she had nothing to lose by being direct. "She was pretty down. She told me you were...involved with someone else."

He drew back a bit, looking startled. "Rayne, I—."

"Oh, I totally forgot about the dessert!" She set her wine glass on the coffee table and started to stand, grateful for the distraction, but he put his hand on her arm to stop her. With a little tug, he brought her back down, and this time their knees were touching.

"Crystal is right," he said in a low voice. "I am interested in someone else."

Rayne suddenly felt the overpowering need to turn on a lamp. To do anything rather than stay in this romantic setting while Chase told her about the woman he was sleeping with. But he was looking at her so intently that she couldn't move away.

"Lucky girl," she said softly, in spite of herself.

Chase smiled a slow, sexy grin that spread pleasure through her whole body. "I'm glad you think so."

He reached out and gently turned her face a little more toward him. Then he leaned in and kissed her, barely pressing his lips against hers with his fingers lingering under her chin.

Rayne froze, thoroughly confused, and Chase pulled back, looking equally confused.

"Did I make a mistake?" he asked.

She jumped to her feet, eager to put some space between them. "No. I mean, yes. I mean, obviously I'm attracted to you, but I can't get involved with you when you're sleeping with someone else."

"Rayne," he said, and he was smiling as he looked up at her. "I didn't want to tell Crystal, but you're the one I'm interested in."

"Oh," she said, feeling foolish. And then when it sank in, "Oh!"

He stood up, just inches away from her. "I know that Colin and Savannah aren't exactly keen on us seeing each other, and

I've tried to stay away, I really have. But..."

"But what?" she asked, her voice catching in her throat, barely able to breathe.

He put one hand on her bare arm and cupped the other one against her neck, his thumb grazing her lips. He leaned close and whispered. "But I can't."

Then his mouth was on hers, and this time there was nothing gentle or tentative about the way he kissed her and thrust his hands in her hair. Rayne stretched toward him, her tongue hungrily seeking his as she breathed in the scent of him. Something inside her, something she'd been holding onto tightly, finally slipped loose. And she couldn't—wouldn't—call it back.

He wrapped his arms around her and pulled her body more tightly against his, and she melted a little more. She pulled back to catch her breath, but he responded by kissing the corner of her mouth and then her chin and jaw, down to her neck, and she was breathing hard.

She wanted him now, here, in this moment, and it felt good to give into her desire. She let go of all the planning she'd been doing for work and all the energy she'd been putting into resisting her attraction. To be alive and touching him in this moment was so damn good that she decided it would be worth whatever penalty she'd have to pay. Tomorrow. Which was worlds away.

Chase covered her mouth with his and reached down to grab her ass, snugging her up against his crotch. Rayne felt the effect she was having on him and ran her hands down his back, feeling the movement of his muscles like a low volt of electricity.

His mouth moved to her neck and his fingers started to undo the top button of her blouse, and she didn't stop him as he worked his way through the next two buttons. But when his warm hand slipped inside her shirt, she took hold of his wrist, suddenly wanting to slow the pace. If she was going to give herself permission to do this, she was going to make it last, savor it like a good meal. An exquisite, one-time-only meal.

He looked at her with a question in his eyes but let her push him back onto the couch. She straddled his lap and pinned his arm back by the wrist, kissing him roughly like a little nip from a playful animal.

"What's the rush?" she whispered in his ear and was rewarded with a shiver.

"Careful you don't start something you can't finish," he murmured as he slipped his arm free of her hands and pulled her head down toward his and kissed her deeply.

After a moment, she pressed her hands against his chest and sat back. Then she started to undo the rest of her blouse one tortuously slow button at a time. When he reached up to help her, she shook her head. "No touching."

Chase's hands dropped to her hips, and his gaze strayed to the hollow between her breasts and her white lacy bra. Then he looked up at her face. "Are you seriously asking me to keep my hands off that body?"

"Mmmm-hmmm," she murmured. "For now at least."

She slid her blouse off her shoulders and let it fall to the floor. His breath caught as he inhaled sharply, and then she leaned forward and started kissing him, long and hot and full of hunger. She pressed her chest against his, and he kept his hands loose against her hips and kissed her back with a ferocious animal hunger that matched her own.

She tugged at his shirt hem and pulled it up, and he immediately raised his arms so she could yank it over his head. She tossed it aside and ran her fingertips across his chest and paused on the tattoo of a Japanese kanji symbol near his left shoulder.

"Let me guess," she said. "Adventure."

He pulled her toward him, abandoning the no-touching rule, and she thrilled to the warmth of his bare skin against hers.

"Don't tell me you read Japanese," he said, nuzzling her ear.

"No, just you."

His mouth found her neck, and he kissed and sucked and she threw her head back so he could have it all, an act of surrender that felt like power. She couldn't believe how amazing it felt to assert her desires in this way. She shifted her weight and pressed herself against his crotch, and he sat forward and wrapped his arms around her and kissed her hard on the mouth.

"You're seriously testing the limits of my control," he said, his voice gruff with desire.

Rayne stopped moving and smiled. "Well, then, I guess we better take a step back."

She stood, and he grabbed her hand, but she pulled free. "We haven't had dessert."

"You're the only dessert I want," he said.

She walked away toward the kitchen, feeling herself wet and swollen and alive for the first time in months. She took the cream puffs out of the fridge and turned to find Chase leaning against the door frame, studying her. The light from the refrigerator cast strange shadows over his face, and he was looking at her with a raw desire that almost made her lose her resolve to go slow.

But she was determined to do this on her own terms. That way, when it all fell apart, she could at least feel like she'd made her own decisions. It gave her a sense of power that was almost as arousing as the sight of him bare-chested in her kitchen.

She picked up the box of pastries and went back to the living room, grabbing his hand as she passed. She led him back to the couch and sat him down.

"Close your eyes," she commanded, and he instantly obeyed.

She straddled him again and took one of the cream puffs and scooped out some of the creamy filling and then put her finger to his lips. He opened his mouth and began sucking the filling off her finger, and they both moaned with pleasure. Then she kissed him, long and deep, before feeding him another scoopful of the filling, sitting back on his thighs with his hands warm and snug against her hips.

"Remember, no peeking," she said as she slid onto the floor.

She knelt between his knees and traced his muscled abs with her tongue as her fingers moved across his pecs and nipples then back down to his stomach, where she grazed the hot, hard erection pressing against his jeans. Chase's sharp intake of breath made her smile, and she was impressed that he kept his promise not to peek. She undid her bra and dropped it to the floor and climbed back into his lap. She reached for his hand and cupped it to bare her breast and held it there while she leaned forward and kissed his neck.

"Oh god," he said, his fingers closing possessively over her breast.

Then he twisted around and had her flat on her back in one effortless move. He hovered over her, looking at her half-naked body in the moonlight for a long moment until she stretched up her hands to touch his chest.

"My turn," he said, catching her wrists and guiding her arms up above her head. "Eyes closed."

Her heart was hammering in anticipation, and a moment later, she felt pastry filling on her lips and opened them to suck the sweet cream off his fingers, moaning in delight. A second later she felt something cold between her breasts, and then he was licking and sucking the creamy filling from her skin. She kicked her heels against the couch cushions and writhed until he finally closed his mouth over her nipple and sucked hard. She arched her back, and he slid one hand under her to guide her toward him and planted kisses in a line from her breastbone to the waistband of her skirt.

She kept her eyes closed, her body alive with sensation as she anticipated what he would do next. He caught both her wrists in one hand and pinned them above her head as kissed her hard on the mouth and then his mouth was on her neck, hot and ravenous and moving lower to enclose each nipple in turn.

"Chase," she moaned.

Then her eyes flew open and they both went still at the sound of footsteps on the front porch.

"Are you expecting anyone?" he whispered.

"No," she whispered back.

Whoever it was knocked on the door, which was a relief because it meant it wasn't Carol or Savannah.

"Is the door locked?" Chase asked.

She tried to remember, but it seemed like ages ago since he'd walked in, fully clothed and a virtual stranger. "I don't know."

He grinned. "Well, someone could get an eyeful," he said as

he unzipped her skirt and slowly, quietly pulled it down away from her hips.

"What are you doing?" she protested.

Without answering, he pushed her panties aside and slipped a finger inside her. She let out a yelp of surprise and pleasure, and he cupped his other hand lightly over her mouth. He leaned close, his finger going even deeper inside her, and she groaned but it was muffled by his hand.

"Shhhhhh," he whispered, his breath hot against her ear.

Rayne felt herself getting wetter and realized she'd never wanted a man so much in her life. She flicked her tongue against the palm of his hand, which was still across her mouth, and he pressed down a little harder, and she licked and tugged at his skin with her teeth until he let out a low moan.

She heard the sound of retreating footsteps outside, and he took his hand away from her mouth.

"Upstairs," she said breathlessly.

"I'm not sure I'm ready," he teased even as he let her slide out from under him.

"Well," she said with a sly smile, as she stood up. "I don't want to make you do anything before you're ready."

Standing in nothing but her panties, she held her hand out to him. Chase stayed where he was, taking her in, his eyes moving over her like a caress. "Goddamn, you are breathtaking," he said.

She pulled him to his feet and kissed his chest as she unhooked his belt then unbuttoned his jeans. He dug his fingers in her hair and tried to control his breathing as she slid his zipper down. She shoved his pants down his hips, careful to keep his boxers in place, and he exhaled in a slow hiss. After he'd stepped out of his jeans, she pushed him down on the couch and straddled him. He started to put his arms around her, but she shook her head.

"Uh-uh. No touching. Remember?"

She lowered herself onto him until she met his erection through the thin cotton of her panties. She started to rock, slowly at first, holding her body up and away from him, and watching him watching her, mesmerized. His gaze flicked from her face to her bare breasts to her crotch, and it was as thrilling as being caressed by him. She threw her head back and danced and bucked, never losing contact.

"Ready yet?" she asked, looking him in the eye.

"I've never been more ready for anything in my life," he said.

He put his arms around her and stood up, and she wrapped her legs around his hips and let him lift her as she forced her tongue between his teeth, smiling at the sharp intake of breath and the growl in his throat.

She swung her feet down to the floor and took him by the hand then led him up the stairs slowly, turning around to kiss him every few steps and gently lifting his fingers away when they reached for her breast or hip. When they got to her bedroom, the moonlight was shining in through the open blinds brightly enough that she could see his face, flushed with desire. She grabbed a condom from her nightstand drawer, and he took it from her without a word. By the time she had stripped off her panties and laid down on the bed, he was naked and ready.

She had a brief view of his gorgeous body before he joined her on the bed, and they collided in a tangle of arms and legs and he was inside her before she knew it. She breathed out a startled "oh!" at the explosion of pleasure that coursed through her body. Then he rolled onto his back, pulling her on top of him, and drew her face in for a kiss before gently pushing her upright.

She smiled down at him as she rocked and twisted, and he squeezed her breasts and then pressed a finger to that hot button of desire, which only made her writhe more wildly against him, harder and faster until she let out a shriek and her whole body shuddered as she exploded in wave after wave of pleasure. She rocked against him hard, and he met her motion for motion until he bucked up against her, growled, "Oh god," and let go inside her.

She felt the hot release and collapsed against his chest. He wrapped his arms around her, brushed the hair from her face, and kissed her gently on the lips, breathing in deeply as though to inhale the scent of her.

"That was even more amazing than I imagined," he said.

"Oh?" she teased as she snuggled against him. "Have you spent a lot of time imagining this?"

"As a matter of fact, I have." He ran his hand lightly down her bare arm then brought her fingers to his lips and kissed them.

"How long?" she asked as she nuzzled his neck.

He paused. "Since at least an hour ago."

She swatted at his chest, and he pulled her tighter, and she suddenly felt all the fatigue and tension drain away. She was totally at ease lying naked beside him and not even interested in what the morning would bring.

She dozed off in his arms and awoke moments, maybe hours later. It was still dark out, and his hand was warm against her stomach and his breath was hot on her neck and then she was kissing him and he was kissing her back. They made love again, hot and fast. The third time, they slowed down.

Chapter 9

Chase opened his eyes to sunlight streaming in through an unfamiliar window. In a second, it all came back to him—the whole glorious night. He'd been with his share of women, but nothing had ever come close to what he'd experienced with Rayne last night. Grinning as he pondered round four, he rolled over to snuggle her, but she wasn't there.

The door was wide open, and he could hear her moving around downstairs so he got up and pulled on his boxers. On his way down, he found his jeans slung over the railing and paused to put them on. He continued into the living room, where he found his shirt draped across the back of the couch. He pulled it on as he headed for the kitchen, where Rayne had her back to him as she filled a tea kettle at the sink.

"Morning, sexy," he said from the doorway, his voice hoarse with sleep.

She squeaked in surprise and spun around to face him.

"I didn't hear you get up," she said.

She was wearing a yellow terrycloth bathrobe, and he was wondering what, if anything, she was wearing under it. Intent on finding out, he started to move toward her, but when she quickly turned back to the sink, he felt a little flicker of uncertainty and stopped.

"Everything OK?" he asked.

"Yeah, of course. It's fine," she said as she turned on the burner under the kettle. "We're all out of coffee, but I've got tea. And eggs. Unless you'd prefer some leftover quiche. I could heat it up—"

As she babbled, Chase closed the distance between them in a few strides, put his hands on her shoulders, and turned her toward him. Then he kissed her on the lips.

"Chase, I think we—"

"Could I take you out to dinner tonight?" he asked as he linked his hands loosely around her waist.

"You mean, like a date?"

Chase looked down at her flushed face and tousled hair and fought the urge to scoop her up and take her right back to bed.

"Well, yeah. That's what people do when they're dating," he said, tucking her hair behind her ear. "They go on dates."

"Are we dating?"

"I certainly hope so."

She stepped away from him, and his heart went a little cold because she wouldn't look him in the eye.

"It just feels...weird," she said.

"What does?" he asked, trying to keep his voice steady.

"Not being able to tell my best friend that I hooked up with an amazing guy because I know she won't be happy for me." She glanced at him and then away. "It makes me think this isn't a good idea."

He fought to keep his frustration in check. He ached to touch her, but he sensed that would be the wrong move. Instead, he leaned a little sideways to put himself in her field of vision.

"This is between you and me, Rayne. It's got nothing to do with Savannah or Colin or Crystal or anyone else. Just you and me."

She smiled but still managed to look sad. And tired. "I wish it were as easy for me as it is for you."

He straightened up, and she must have seen the hurt in his face because she rushed to continue. "I wasn't trying to insult you. I just meant that our friends aren't as important to you as they are to me. Oh god, I'm making it worse."

He started to back away. "If you're regretting last night, just say so."

She put her hand on his arm. "No, I don't regret it. I'm just thinking maybe we should take it slow."

He gazed at her, thinking slow could be good, he could work with that, when the tea kettle burst into a high-pitched whistle. She moved away from him to turn off the burner. He followed and put his arms around her from behind and hugged her to him, kissing her ear. To his surprise and pleasure, she relaxed back into him.

"We can go as slow as you want," he said, nuzzling her neck. "All I ask is that you give it a chance before you make up your mind. And that you leave everyone else out of it."

She twisted around in his arms to face him, looking much friendlier now. "Fair enough. But I'm having dinner with Savannah tonight."

He smiled. "Then another night. Whenever you want."

"OK."

"And what are we doing about Savlin?" he asked, using the merged version of Savannah's and Colin's names that drove them crazy.

She smiled but didn't answer right away. Instead, she studied him for a long moment, and his heart beat a little faster, afraid of what her answer might be and wishing he knew how to read her expressions better.

"I say we keep this between us for now," she said. "And cool things off until we get through this fundraiser. OK?"

He nodded slowly. Waiting wouldn't be easy, especially since it was making whatever was going on between them start to feel like more than a fling, but he didn't want to think about that now. He had something more pressing on his mind.

"You mean cool things off starting tomorrow, right?" He tilted her face up and kissed her on the mouth, letting his hand stray to the belt of her bathrobe.

"Chase—" she started to say, but he gave the belt a tug and slipped his hand inside. He felt bare skin and breathed in with a sigh—and smiled when he heard the breath catch in her throat.

"Breakfast in bed?" he asked in a soft voice.

A thrill went through him when she put her arms around his neck and whispered yes in his ear.

A couple hours later, they stood in the living room, fully clothed, and Rayne wrapped her arms around Chase for a good-bye kiss.

"Still a hard no on dinner tonight?" he asked as he slid his hands down to squeeze her ass through the snug yoga pants she'd tossed on before walking him to the door. "That thing I did before, with the swirl and the biting, that didn't change your answer by any chance?"

Rayne grinned and kissed his jaw. "Sorry, no. But if you keep working on it, maybe next time—" She yelped in surprise as Chase suddenly picked her up.

"You didn't seem to think it needed work an hour ago," he said as pressed her up against the wall next to the door then let her slide down the length of his body until her feet touched the floor.

Laughing, Rayne wrapped her arms around his waist.

"But I do like the part where you talk about next time," he said, brushing her hair behind her ear.

Her face turned a serious. "Me, too. But we agreed to wait until after the gala, remember?"

Chase nodded slowly. "I'll do my best to keep my hands— and mouth—off you until then."

"It's only three weeks," Rayne reminded him as she ushered him out the door.

"I'll be counting the days," Chase called over his shoulder as he walked down the porch steps.

Three weeks was a hell of a long time to wait, and he didn't want things to go cold between them, so Chase took every opportunity to keep the heat simmering. A few days later, he stopped by her office to take some photos of the building, and afterward, he walked into her office and shut the door behind him and swept her up into a kiss before she could protest. And though she was shocked at first, she kissed him back, and he was seriously wondering whether her bathroom door had a lock on it when she finally broke away.

"Is that you cooling things off?" she asked as she tried to put her hair and clothes back in order.

He leaned against the edge of her desk and watched her. "You and I might have different definitions of 'cool.' And you look fine, by the way. Better than fine." He reached for her hand, but she snatched it away at the sound of someone knocking and then opening the door.

Sheila stood in the doorway. "Oh, I'm sorry! I didn't realize you were busy."

Chase said, "It's fine. I was just leaving. I'll email you the photos I just took, Rayne." Then he winked, she blushed, and he sauntered out the door. Mission accomplished.

A week later, Rayne stopped by Zipped to talk to Colin about the catering for the gala and was a little thrilled—and nervous—when she spotted Chase at the far end of the bar. He waved hello, and she responded with what she hoped was a friendly but casual smile. She'd specifically come in the early afternoon when Savannah would still be at work. Rayne had been avoiding her as much as possible because she wouldn't be able to lie if Savannah asked a direct question, and Savannah always knew when Rayne had a secret.

Now she realized that if Colin figured it out, it would be the same as telling Savannah but worse because she'd be hearing it from Colin. Rayne's head was spinning, and she prayed that Chase would keep his promise and behave himself.

"Rayne! Where have you been hiding?" Colin asked as he slapped a cocktail napkin in front of her and started fixing her a club soda with lime.

"Hiding? Why would I be hiding?" Rayne asked with a nervous laugh.

Behind Colin's back, Chase caught her eye, gave a little shake of his head, and mouthed the word "relax." She took a deep breath and reached into her bag for her notebook.

"Have you had lunch yet?" Colin asked, standing poised at the register.

"No, but—"

"No buts. Kale and cranberry salad with organic chicken sound good?"

Knowing it was useless to protest, Rayne nodded. After Colin finished typing in her order, he came over and leaned on the bar in front of her and said, "All right, hit me. What do you need and how much of it do you need?"

"I can't tell you how much we appreciate you donating all the food," she said. "It's going to be a huge piece of why this event is successful."

Colin waved away the compliment. "Just give me the numbers, kid. I can't let my good-for-nothing brother contribute more than me to this event. I have a reputation to uphold."

From down the bar, Chase called out a muffled "Hey!" around a mouthful of burger. Colin ignored him, keeping his eyes on Rayne.

"Well, we're estimating about two hundred people, although we can give you firmer numbers in about a week," she said, consulting her notes. "We'd like a bar and appetizer stations spread throughout the house to make sure people move around and see everything. Crystal is going to provide the desserts and coffee service, so you don't have to worry about that."

Colin pulled out his phone and typed some notes into it. "Got it! Consider it done."

As he pushed himself back from the bar, Diana came up behind him and handed him Rayne's salad.

"Savannah's going to be at your place tonight because I have a late meeting, just FYI," Colin said as he set the salad and silverware in front of her. "I know you guys haven't had much girl time lately."

He winked at her before he moved off down the bar to attend to other customers.

Rayne felt a stab of guilt. She'd love nothing more than to hang out with Savannah tonight, but that would spell trouble in the secret-keeping department so it looked like she'd be working late again.

She ate her salad quickly, checking her email on her phone and trying not to watch Chase as he finished his meal and bantered with Diana and Colin.

Chase had nearly choked on his burger Rayne walk into Zipped. He'd always had a physical response to the sight of her.

But since they'd made love, the experience had intensified, and he'd stopped at the bar after the lunch rush specifically because he thought it reduced his chances of running into her. Business was slow at that hour, and Colin had been giving him a hard time about being involved with a secret woman, though his only evidence was that Chase always had a woman, and if he wasn't talking, then it was obviously a secret woman. And then Rayne had walked in and he'd nearly lost it.

Chase couldn't let her leave without at least talking to her, but if he went to sit next to her, Colin would pick up on their chemistry in a heartbeat. He was debating waiting for her outside when Diana came to take his plate and whispered, "Stare any harder and you'll burn a hole through her."

"I don't what you're talking about," he said, suppressing a smile as he sat back in his chair and stretched his arms over his head.

"I knew you liked adventure, but I didn't think you had a death wish," she said with a shake of her head.

"D, I seriously don't know what you're talking about."

"Mmmm-hmmm," Diana murmured. "You're just lucky your brother isn't as observant as I am because the moment she walked in, everything about you changed. You practically started to glow."

Chase frowned. "You're out of your mind. I'm a man. I don't glow. It's a biological impossibility."

"What is a biological impossibility?" Colin asked as he joined Diana behind the bar.

"For a man to glow," Chase said.

"Oh please," Diana said. "Colin's been glowing since the first day Savannah walked in here!"

"I have?" Colin said, looking down at his hands as though he had something on him.

"Ah, yeah, now I see what you mean. Guys can glow. It's like a pinkish tint, right?" Chase teased and dodged the napkin Colin threw at him.

Laughing, Diana started to walk away.

"You really think I'm glowing?" Colin asked Chase.

Diana caught Chase's eye and called, "Hey, Colin, I could use your help in the kitchen for a second."

Colin turned to join her, and Chase flashed her a grateful smile. He stood up just as Rayne slid down from her chair and headed for the door. He caught up with her outside.

"Let me walk you back to your office," he said.

"Somehow I don't think I have a choice," she said with a smile.

"No, you don't. Besides, I have kept things cool for a whole week, so I ought to get some sort of reward."

She gave him a quick kiss on the cheek.

"Sweet," he said, "but not exactly what I had in mind."

She giggled, and he took her by the hand and pulled her into a shadowy, narrow alleyway, where he kissed her on the mouth and planted both hands firmly on her ass.

"Better," he murmured as he nuzzled her neck.

He had to admit he was liking the furtiveness of their relationship. He'd always simply gone after the women he wanted, but somehow not being able to openly pursue Rayne made him crave her even more. The anticipation was a sweet sort of agony. And she seemed to be excited by it, too—if the shine in those smoky gray eyes was any indication.

"Are you free for dinner Saturday?" he asked.

"Chase, we agreed—"

"It's just dinner," he interrupted. "If we go someplace out of the way, no one has to know. I could promise to keep my hands to myself, but we both know I'd be lying."

He was pleased when she smiled in response. She had that sexy glow that women got when they knew a man wanted them. It made him want her even more.

"All right," she said.

"Great! Meet me at the Eastern Market metro at 6. We're taking a ride to the suburbs."

He walked her the rest of the way to her office without touching her.

"See you Saturday," he said and watched her walk up the front steps like a man under a spell.

When he got back to Zipped, he found Diana clearing one of the tables and said, "Thanks."

"For what?" she asked with feigned innocence. "I needed to talk to Colin about a liquor order."

He laughed. "Well, I appreciate your timing."

Diana shrugged, still not acknowledging she did anything on purpose. "Keeping your thing with Rayne on the down-low?"

"Yeah, for now."

"Kind of like having an affair with a married woman," Diana said. "Sex is always way hotter when you think you might get caught."

Chase smiled. "Absolutely." He was thinking of that first night on Rayne's couch when someone had knocked on the door.

Diana shook her head. "I don't even want to know what that grin is about."

On Saturday night, Rayne and Chase rode the silver line out to Tysons Corner in the suburbs of Virginia and ate a fancy chain steakhouse where they were sure not to run into anyone they knew. They sat at the bar and talked and laughed and brushed against each other. Rayne was a little reserved at first, but by the time they finished the appetizers, she was resting her hand on his thigh, and they were just two people out on a date with nothing to hide.

On the ride back into town, they sat in the last seat on the last car and made out like teenagers all the way back to her stop at Eastern Market. He got off the train with her then pulled her close and kissed her on the mouth.

"That was fun," he said. "I feel like I'm having an affair with a married woman."

She drew back. "How is that a good thing?"

"It adds spice, don't you think?" He ran his hand down her back and rested it on her ass. "And don't act all shocked and horrified. You're enjoying it, too." He started kissing her neck, and when she tried to twist away, he held her tighter.

"Run away with me," he said, channeling Humphrey Bogart

in an old black-and-white movie. "Just leave the bastard and come away with me."

Rayne struggled weakly in his arms, and he was going to let her go, thinking she wasn't into the joke, when she said, "But I can't. He would just die without me. Can't you see? It's no good between us!"

He planted sloppy kisses all over her face. "You must. He doesn't deserve you, kid! I'll kill myself without you. I swear it."

She laughed so hard that she could hardly catch her breath.

"You're nuts," she said.

"It's your fault, you know. It's that perfume, it's the way your ass sways ever so slightly when you walk, it's that neck of yours. But mostly it's your smart, beautiful, mesmerizing eyes."

She had stopped laughing and was staring at him, her gray eyes wide.

"You make me crazy," he said and immediately realized that he'd gone farther than he'd intended. But he wouldn't take it back either.

A train pulled into the station, and he started to walk backward away from her down the platform as it slowed to a stop beside him. She was still watching him, dumbfounded.

"Don't say a word," he said, back in character. "I want to remember you just this way. He won, dammit. And I don't know how I'll go on without you."

He jumped on the train, and the doors slid shut.

Chapter 10

Rayne walked home from the metro station on that balmy Saturday evening feeling bewildered. In all their goofing around on the platform, Chase had said something that almost sounded like a declaration of love. And it had caught her off-guard.

She had been thoroughly enjoying their time together, and she had to admit the secretiveness made her heart beat a little faster and made their stolen kisses a little more intense. She was looking forward to seeing where things would go after the gala, and he seemed to be thinking the same thing.

But his comment about feeling like he was having an affair with a married woman had brought her up short. It made her think about Brandon, which she didn't like to do. Brandon had been on the board of CACC at the time and said he wanted to keep their relationship a secret because in some technical, distant way he was her boss, and it might look inappropriate.

She'd thought it was a bit of a stretch even then, but it wasn't until she found out he was married that she realized his true motivation for not wanting Jeremy to know they were seeing each other and never having her over to his house in Annapolis.

She broke things off as soon as she found out—called and told him she knew about his wife and it was over. He kept calling her, though she never returned his calls and finally switched phone companies and numbers (she needed to update her phone anyway, she told herself). And the fact that he never showed up at her door to beg her forgiveness and say he'd left his wife for her was all the proof she needed that their relationship hadn't meant as much to him as it had to her.

Their fling had only lasted a couple of months, but it had been intense. For days afterward she couldn't take long enough, hot enough showers in a desperate attempt to wash away the shame and guilt. And heartbreak.

The idea that somehow her relationship with Chase paralleled what she'd done with Brandon made her want to take a step back. She was glad they'd agreed to wait until after the gala. As she reached her front door, she was equally glad that she'd gone ahead and booked a room at the swanky Willard hotel for the night of the gala. She hadn't told him because she wanted it to be a surprise. The thought of leading him through that ornate lobby in his tuxedo was enough to get her pulse racing. She imagined kissing him in the elevator on the way up to their room and then peeling his tux off piece by piece as she made love to every inch of his incredible body.

She was also looking forward to finally telling Savannah. Between Rayne's near-total absorption in planning for the gala and Savannah spending time with Colin whenever she could, it had been easy enough to avoid the topic of Chase. And once Savannah saw how hard Chase had worked on Rayne's behalf and learned that they'd been building a friendship, Rayne was sure her friend would be happy for her.

Rayne only had to wait one more week to bring everything out in the open. As she climbed up the stairs to her bedroom, her phone beeped with a text message from Chase and she imagined him saying it in his forties movie-star voice: *Good night, my darling.*

The next day, Chase wanted to keep the movie fantasy going with Rayne over texts and was trying to figure out how a 1940s film star would reference sex in a classy way when his phone rang, and he recognized the number of Ben's contact.

"What's up?" Chase asked.

"We finally got the OK from the Nepalese government. My writer, Roy Fellows, will be in Kathmandu in three days. How soon can you be on a flight?"

"In three days," Chase said.

"Great. I'll email you his contact info and travel details so you guys can coordinate."

"Fantastic!" Chase said. "I really appreciate the opportunity."

He put down his cell phone and started pulling out camera equipment and rooting through his dresser, and it wasn't until he finally turned up his passport that it dawned on him. Today was Sunday, the gala was this coming Saturday, so if he left in three days...

He was going to miss the gala.

He stood still in the middle of the room, clothes strewn across the bed, camera gear everywhere. Rayne will understand, he told himself, wishing it felt true.

He sank down on the edge of the bed. He needed the gig, he needed the money, and he needed to travel...right? He suddenly realized that he hadn't had that itch for an airport in a couple weeks. Ever since he'd slept with Rayne.

He stood up abruptly and paced around the room, raking his hands through his hair. He'd be back in a month tops, and he and Rayne could pick up right where they left off.

"It'll be fine!" he said out loud, even though he knew he was fooling himself.

He felt pulled in two different directions, and he didn't like it. He didn't like the idea of telling her he was going overseas when she was counting on him to be at the gala. But he also didn't like the idea of saying he couldn't take the gig because his secret girlfriend would be mad.

She'd have to understand. He'd make her understand. The trick would be in the telling. While he was trying to figure out a way to tell her that didn't end with her saying she should have listened to Savannah and Colin, his cell phone rang. He didn't recognize the number but thought it might be the writer on the Nepal assignment.

But it wasn't Roy Fellows. The man on the other end of the line said his name was Brandon Wallace.

"I hope you don't mind, but I got your number from your mother. I received her invitation to the fundraiser for the Center for Action on Climate Change, and I saw that the point of contact is Rayne Michael. I was hoping you could put me in touch with her."

Chase was a little irritated. "Her contact info is on the invitation," he said.

"There's just an email address, and I was really hoping to talk to her. We used to work together, but I lost touch with her."

Chase hesitated. He didn't like giving out other people's cell phone numbers. "I can give you her office number."

"Do you have her cell phone number? I haven't been able to catch her at the office. I was planning on making a pretty big donation, and I'd really like to talk to her about how else I might help."

Chase looked around at his chaotic room. His head was starting to hurt, and he just wanted to get the guy off the phone.

"Yeah, sure," he said and gave him Rayne's number.

"I can't thank you enough," the guy said, sounding way more excited than a simple phone number would warrant.

As Chase set his phone down, he remembered something Rayne had said about not dating men she worked with... anymore. For a brief moment, Chase wondered if he should be jealous. Then he decided he was just feeling guilty and paranoid and turned his attention back to the mayhem that surrounded him.

Chase had worked hard to arrange his life to avoid this kind of emotional turmoil. So he decided to use a trick he'd developed for complicated photo shoots or when he was stranded in a remote location: Make a plan of action and then focus on accomplishing one task at a time. He immediately stopped pacing.

Task number one was connecting with the writer. He checked his email and found the message with Roy Fellows' contact information and itinerary. Chase sent him a quick note to say he planned to leave D.C. for Kathmandu on Wednesday and would email his travel details as soon as he had them. He also gave the guy his cell phone number so they could text each other.

Next task was booking a flight. He pulled out his laptop and started researching his options. He found a decent rate on a flight that had a couple short layovers and left Dulles early on

Wednesday morning. With that booked, he sent an email to a guest house where he'd stayed when he was in Kathmandu a couple years ago and reserved a room. And he forwarded all that info to Fellows.

"Done and done!" he said out loud, feeling calmer now and more in control.

Next task: Pack his camera gear. That took a little while because it required being judicious about what he needed but not leaving behind anything he couldn't live without.

Finally, he zipped his camera bag closed and said, "Check!"

Then he gathered his standard travel clothes and packed them in his duffel bag—moisture-wicking shirts, a thermal micro fleece jacket, knit cap, a couple pairs of cargo pants, his trusty hiking boots, a few pairs of socks and boxers, and last but not least, his dry sack to protect everything in case of rain or unexpected river crossings.

He closed the duffel and set it next to his camera bag. The sight of them gave him a feeling of satisfaction and Zen-like calm. Once he threw in some power bars and toiletries, he could live for months if need be out of just those two bags.

But within seconds the feeling of dread and unease crept back in as his thoughts turned to his next task: Tell Rayne. He shoved both bags in the closet and shut the door so Colin wouldn't see the telltale signs of a Chase departure. The last thing he needed was for the news to reach Rayne via the Savlin network.

As if the universe was mocking him, he got an email from his mother asking when he was going to stop by and pick up his tux, which she'd had dry cleaned for him. He didn't dare tell her he wouldn't need it so instead he sent a note saying he'd let her know. Christ, when had his life become so freaking complicated? Restlessly he pulled open the fridge to grab a beer but found only bottled water.

At least with Crystal it had been just the two of them—until he'd broken it off and Colin had to hear about how bummed she was. Those were the days, Chase thought bitterly. His desire to simply disappear was starting to grow.

He loved airports, loved the anticipation and freedom of getting on a plane and winding up someplace far away and different. He loved wandering around a foreign country and getting to know the culture by stopping people and pointing to his camera and, if he didn't know at least a little of the local language, miming that he wanted to take their picture. Children especially were all smiles when he asked, but even adults often shyly grinned while he took a photo and then crowded around to look at themselves on the preview screen of his camera.

He'd done that in cities and villages all over the world, and his tall, well-fed American body and shaggy hair attracted attention wherever he went. At times like those, he was a man without ties, without obligations, without the ability to disappoint people. He wouldn't trade the experience for all the stability in the world. But, it suddenly occurred to him as he leaned against the kitchen counter and drained a bottle of water that he did have stability in his life. He had his family and his apartment with Colin and the promise of a steady income if he ever needed it. He could go off and have his adventures and come back home and get cleaned up and rested and then go out and do it again. He'd never really seen it that way before, and now that he did, he had a sudden worry that it might all go away.

As he tossed the empty water bottle into the recycling bin, his phone dinged and he looked down to see a message from Rayne: *Were you going to drop your photos off ahead of time or bring them the night of the gala?*

His heart sank. He'd abruptly dropped the fun, sexy banter they'd had going that morning when he got the call about Nepal and now she was clearly back onto business. He had planned to pick up his prints from the framing shop on Tuesday anyway. It was one thing to skip out on the gala, it was another to bail on his donation. He could drop them by her office that afternoon, ask her to go for a walk, and explain everything. That gave him two days to come up with a plan. And two days to avoid seeing her until he did.

Finally he typed back: *I'll drop them off ahead of time,* and left it at that.

He sat down to make a quick list of the things he'd need to buy before he left, and after several minutes, she texted back: *Everything OK?*

Yeah, great! he replied.

A couple minutes later, she texted: *I'm really looking forward to the gala—and what happens after.* Followed by a grinning emoji.

He stared out the window for a long time. It was starting to rain, and people were pulling up collars and popping open umbrellas and dashing under overhangs to avoid getting wet. Finally he typed back, *Me too.* He hated himself for not telling her the truth. And he realized that Colin had been right all along: Chase didn't deserve her.

Chapter 11

With the gala only days away, Rayne took Monday afternoon off and rode the subway to Dupont Circle to meet Savannah outside her office. After a quick lunch, they walked to a little boutique nearby to pick out a dress for Rayne to wear to the event.

She tried on a dizzying number of dresses, and they decided against floor-length (too formal) and stiff tulle (too ballerina-like). She also rejected a dress that was too snug and short—though Savannah swore it was custom made for her—because she didn't think it looked professional enough. But she couldn't help fantasizing about coming back to buy it for a date night with Chase at some point.

They finally zeroed in on a knee-length dress of beaded lace in dove gray with a tastefully plunging V-neck and sheer three-quarter sleeves. Savannah checked the price tag as Rayne studied herself in the mirror.

"It's gorgeous and totally perfect, but it's a little pricey, Rayney," she said. "We could keep looking if you want."

Rayne liked the way the dress complemented her eyes. It was classy with just the right hint of sexy.

"It's a special night," she said. In more ways than Savannah knew. "I think I'll go for it."

"Good!" Savannah said with a smile. "You deserve it!"

Rayne picked out a pair of matching shoes that had a heel at a height she could manage to walk on for hours. She thought about taking a photo of herself in the dress and sending it to Chase—a glimpse of what he could look forward to on Saturday night—but she didn't know how to explain that to Savannah. So she changed back into her street clothes and was walking to the counter to check out when her phone rang. She hoped it was Chase—she'd barely heard from him in the past twenty-four hours—but her excitement faded at the sight of an unfamiliar number.

"Hello?" she said, cradling the phone to her ear as she set the dress and shoes on the counter, smiling an apology to the saleswoman at the register.

"Rayne? Hi! It's Brandon."

She nearly dropped the phone. "Brandon?"

Savannah looked up in alarm.

"Listen, before you say anything," he said, talking fast, "I got an invitation from Bea Allison for CACC's fundraiser, and I want to help."

"My email address is on the invitation," Rayne said and held the phone away to click the off button and end the call.

"Wait—please don't hang up!" he said.

She brought the phone back up to her ear. "Give me one good reason why I shouldn't."

"Because your landlord, Vincent, owes me a favor. I've already talked to him about lowering the price for the house to make it more affordable for CACC. And I am prepared to match whatever money you raise Saturday night toward a down payment."

She paused. That was definitely a reason.

"Thank you," she finally said.

"I'd like to go over the details with you in person."

"I should have known—"

"Please give me a chance. I just want to have a cup of coffee and talk about the fundraiser. I might be able to help in other ways."

"You're already being generous enough," she said. "I'll have Jeremy get in touch with you."

"No, Jeremy is... well, we're not on the best of terms since I left the board, and I think it would be better if the offer came through you."

She briefly wondered if their falling out had had anything to do with her. Brandon had left the board shortly after their breakup—in the middle of his term. Maybe Jeremy had been pissed about it. Or maybe he'd found out about the affair...?

"Just meet me for a cup of coffee," Brandon said. "Not for me, for CACC."

"All right," Rayne said. "Tomorrow at 4:00. There's a place called Sweet Happens a couple of blocks from CACC."

"I'll be there," he said. "And thank you."

And then she remembered that she'd switched her cell phone number after she'd broken it off with him.

"By the way, how did you get my phone number?" she asked.

"Bea put me in touch with her son Chase, and he gave me your number."

"He did?" She was going to have to have a chat with Chase— as soon as she could figure out how to do it without revealing that she'd had an affair with a married man.

"See you tomorrow," Brandon said. "I'm looking forward to it."

Rayne clicked the disconnect button without comment and tried to ignore Savannah's stare as she tucked her phone back in her purse.

"Did I just hear you making plans to meet Brandon Wallace for coffee tomorrow?" Savannah said.

"Yes, but it's not what you think."

"Rayney, there is no reason in the world for you to be nice to that man. And please tell me you're not still attracted to him."

"God, no!" Rayne said. "But he heard about the fundraiser, and he said he can get the owner to sell us the house and match whatever we raise, so I have to at least talk to him about it."

"So do it over the phone—or better yet, have Jeremy do it."

"They've had some sort of falling out," Rayne said. "It's just coffee, and I picked Sweet Happens because I figure having Crystal there will keep me grounded."

"Why do you think you'll need grounding?" Savannah asked, eyes narrowed.

Rayne smiled. "I'd rather not go to jail for assaulting the guy. Though now that I think about it, that might totally be worth it."

Savannah laughed and then quickly turned serious. "Please be careful."

"I can handle it," Rayne said.

But she didn't feel nearly as confident as she was acting. In fact, she was already regretting that she'd agreed to meet him. If Chase hadn't given Brandon her number, she could have gone on ignoring him forever. Even if he came to the gala, it would be so busy and crowded that she wouldn't even have to talk to him. Plus, once he realized she was with Chase, Brandon would have backed off.

She knew it wasn't Chase's fault, but she still felt more than a little irritated that he'd been so cavalier about giving her number to anyone who asked for it.

The next day, Rayne managed to keep her mind on work with only a few moments of panic when she remembered that she'd be seeing Brandon later. Finally at 3:45, she grabbed her purse and hurried over to Sweet Happens. She wanted to arrive a couple minutes early and see if she and Crystal could agree on a bailout signal ahead of time.

But when Rayne got there, Brandon was already waiting by the door.

"It's good to see you," he said, smiling a little uncertainly.

If she was objective—if she'd just seen him in passing on the street—she'd think he was a handsome man. He had thick blond hair that fell in a swoop across his forehead, pale blue eyes, and a vaguely Nordic face. He was only a couple inches taller than her, and he was fit and muscular. He'd worked hard building his management consulting company, and he flaunted it by wearing tastefully expensive suits and a Rolex that probably cost more than a year's tuition at George Washington University.

But she was far from objective, and in spite of herself, she felt a flicker of the old attraction. She didn't want to say it was good to see him, too, so instead she said, "I only have half an hour. I've got to get back to the office."

His smile faltered. "Of course. You must be very busy with the gala only a few days away."

He held the door for her, and she caught a whiff of his aftershave as she walked past, a scent she used to treasure when she smelled it on her clothes, in her hair, on her skin after he'd left. And gone home to his wife, she reminded herself.

Crystal was sliding a tray of coconut-frosted cupcakes into the glass case when they walked in. She looked up and smiled at Rayne.

"Hey, how's it going?" she said, then she noticed Brandon and raised her eyebrows at Rayne.

"This is Brandon Wallace, he's a former colleague," Rayne said, hoping she sounded professional and unemotional. "Brandon, this is Crystal."

He reached across the counter to shake Crystal's hand. "It's a pleasure," he said.

"We just want a couple coffees," Rayne said briskly.

Crystal gave her a puzzled look, and Rayne realized she was bordering on rude, but she couldn't help it.

"Sure thing," Crystal said. "Hazelnut OK? Or I've got some Sumatra brewing if you can wait a few minutes."

"Hazelnut is fine," Rayne said.

Crystal grabbed two mugs and started filling them at the coffee dispenser behind the counter. "Could I interest you in a couple of croissants?"

"That sounds delicious," Brandon said.

"Great. I've got some just coming out of the oven. I'll bring everything over to your table."

Rayne reached for her purse, intending to at least pay for her half, but Brandon stopped her. "Let me," he said, handing Crystal a twenty-dollar bill.

She started to punch numbers on the register, and he took a sip of coffee as she got his change. "This is delicious," he said, and Crystal smiled.

Rayne headed for a table in the far corner, where she sat down and took a drink of the coffee, hoping the jolt of caffeine would keep her edgy.

Brandon joined her. "This is a nice place."

"Yeah, it's great," Rayne said, pulling a pad and pen from her bag. "So tell me exactly what Vincent said."

"He agreed to come down five percentage points on the

sale price," he said, sipping his coffee. "My lawyer drafted a document, and Vincent has signed it. I'll email you a copy when I get back to the office. And I'm still prepared to match whatever you raise at the event. I can put that in writing, too."

She set her pen down. "If everything is taken care of, then why are we meeting?"

He took a sip of his coffee and eyed her over the rim of his mug. Then he smiled. "You always were very direct. I've missed that."

When Rayne didn't respond, he sighed and glanced down at his coffee then back up at her. "Yvonne left me."

Rayne stared at him in open-mouthed surprise. "Is that what you wanted to tell me? That your wife finally came to her senses and left you?"

Crystal came over to the table with the croissants, smiling until she got closer and sensed the tension between them.

"Just let me know if you need anything else," she said and hurried back to the counter. Neither of them even looked at the pastries.

Brandon leaned closer and put his hand on Rayne's. She snatched it away.

"Yes, I wanted to tell you about Yvonne," he said in a low voice. "Because it made me realize how much I've missed you."

Rayne sat rigid in her chair. "You've missed me?" she said. "You could have emailed me that news bulletin."

"I've tried email," he said, revealing the first hint of frustration. "You never respond. And you don't return my calls to the office. Yvonne told me she was leaving a month ago, and I've been in a black hole ever since. Until I got that invitation about the gala. And I saw your name on it, and I just... I realized that Yvonne and I had never been right for each other."

"Gee, what was your first clue?" Rayne said. "When you started messing around with younger women?"

He winced. "It wasn't women, plural. It was just you. It's only ever been you." He put his hand flat on the table and leaned toward her. "I was wrong not to fight for you. I never should have let you go."

She sat back, unsure of how to respond. Crystal glanced over as she wiped down the counters and caught Rayne's eye with a look of concern. Rayne nodded slightly to signal that she had this thing under control.

"I'm sorry about your marriage," she said. She'd never met his wife, and she had never wished her ill. Brandon had gotten all her fury. "But Yvonne is better off."

He nodded, looking miserable. "You're absolutely right."

She'd never seen him take responsibility like this. When she'd told him it was over, he had pleaded and tried to convince her that a long-term secret affair was in everyone's best interests. He'd never admitted that he'd done anything wrong. Now in spite of herself, she was softening toward him.

"Look, Brandon, I really appreciate you helping CACC out. And I'm sure you and Jeremy can patch things up—"

"He forced me off the board, you know," Brandon said, his hand gripping the coffee cup. "He found out, or at least he had his suspicions, about us. He was furious. I didn't tell him the truth. I didn't want you to lose your job. But I didn't argue. I left the board instead of making a fuss."

Rayne didn't entirely believe his motivations, but she felt a warm glow toward Jeremy for trying to protect her.

"I should have told him the truth," Brandon said. "I should have told Yvonne. I should have left her then and there so I could be with you."

Rayne rocked back in her seat. He watched her carefully, hopefully. "Will you have dinner with me tomorrow night?"

"Brandon, I don't think—"

"I just want the chance for us to get to know each other again. And then you can decide. I'll leave it all up to you."

She took a deep breath. She glanced up at Crystal again, but a woman came in pushing a stroller, and Crystal was cooing at the baby while the woman decided what to order.

"I'm kind of seeing someone right now," Rayne said.

"Kind of?"

It sounded stupid even to her. "It's...complicated."

"I'll make things easy." He reached into his pocket and pulled out a business card, then he jotted his cell phone number on the back and handed it to her. "Call me anytime, day or night, and we can talk. And dinner is an open invitation." He stood up. "I want you back in my life, Rayne. Whatever it takes."

She watched him walk out the door and then stared at the business card in her hand. Had that just happened? Brandon wanted her back, Yvonne was out of the picture, and Rayne didn't know what to do with any of that information.

Crystal came over to collect their dishes. "Want me to box up the croissants so you can take them home?"

Rayne looked up at her blankly.

"You OK?" Crystal asked. "That looked like a pretty intense conversation."

"Yeah, I'm fine," Rayne said, still feeling dazed. "And sure, I'll take the croissants to go."

Crystal took the dishes back to the counter, and Rayne joined her there. As Crystal boxed up the pastries, she said, "I think I've figured out which painting to give you for the auction. Or at least I've narrowed it down to two."

"I can take both if you like," Rayne said. "If they don't sell, you'll get them back. And if they do, you'll get a bigger tax write-off."

Crystal's smile lit up her whole face, and Rayne felt a twinge of guilt for not telling Crystal that she was seeing Chase. It was sneaky and dirty, and it was starting to remind her of how things had been with Brandon.

"I can't thank you enough for letting me do this," Crystal said.

"I should be thanking you. Seriously, your work is gorgeous," Rayne said. "Just drop the paintings off at the office tomorrow. The address is on the invitation. Will you be at the gala?"

"Wouldn't miss it for the world!"

Rayne smiled and took the box of pastries and headed for the door. She paused outside and sent Savannah a quick text: *Just met with Brandon. We need a girl's night, stat! When will you be home??*

Moments later, she got a response: *Half hour. Is this a wine or a cupcake night?*

Wine. Definitely wine.

On it! See you soon.

Rayne put her phone away and started for home. She had decided to tell Savannah everything, and that decision instantly made her feel better.

Rayne got home fifteen minutes later, and her phone beeped as she set her bag down on the couch. It was a text from Chase: *At your office. Where RU?*

Rayne felt a flash of irritation. He'd barely texted her in the past couple of days, and she hadn't set eyes on him since leaving him at the subway on Saturday night. And now he decided to show up at her office one of the few times she wasn't there.

Home, she texted back. Then added, *I'm telling Savannah.*

Telling her what?

About us. I'm tired of lying. She flopped down on the couch, suddenly feeling exhausted, and stared at her phone.

When he still hadn't replied after three minutes, Rayne felt a rush of anxiety. She jumped up from the couch and stalked into the kitchen, where she pulled out two large wine glasses and fought the urge to text him again. Maybe he was in the bathroom or talking to someone or getting on the subway. Or maybe a giant acorn had fallen on his head and he had amnesia.

She was debating texting Savannah to ask for cupcakes after all when she finally got a response from Chase, but the message only heightened her anxiety: *I need to talk to you first. Heading your way. B there in 5.*

She didn't text him back.

Chapter 12

Savannah walked in the door carrying not one but two bottles of wine, which she set on the coffee table before tossing her bag on the floor and sitting down next to Rayne on the couch.

"You look freaked out," she said. "You never look freaked out. What did Brandon say to you?"

"He told me his wife left him." Rayne was still shaken, but at least she knew what was up with Brandon. She couldn't say the same about Chase. Why did he want her to wait before telling Savannah?

"Let me guess," Savannah said, her voice dripping with sarcasm. "He wants you back?"

Rayne nodded. "He basically admitted that it was all his fault and he should have left her long ago—for me. He said I was the only one he cheated with. And he sounded so...sincere."

"Rayney, this is Brandon Wallace we're talking about—the man who would do or say anything to get what he wants." Savannah stood and carried a bottle of wine into the kitchen while she continued talking. "And right now, he wants a pretty young woman on his arm to show the world how well he's adjusting to his divorce."

Savannah returned with an open bottle and the two glasses, which she promptly filled.

"Wow, you cut right to the chase," Rayne said and immediately wished she'd used another expression. Then she realized it was just the opening she needed.

"Speaking of Chase," she said, her eyes on her wine glass. "There's something I need to tell you."

Savannah raised an eyebrow. "Chase, as in Colin's brother?"

Rayne nodded then stalled by taking a long drink of the sweet white wine. This was proving to be harder than she'd expected. "Remember that weekend last month when I was just starting to plan the gala and Carol was at her conference and you were staying at Colin's?"

Savannah nodded warily, lifting her wine glass and taking a healthy sip. But before Rayne could say she'd made crazy-mad love to Chase and then didn't tell Savannah or anyone else about it, there was a loud knock at the door. Setting her wine glass down and giving Rayne a questioning look, Savannah got up to answer it. Rayne stood up, too, but stayed by the couch.

"Speak of the devil," Savannah said as she held the door open for Chase.

He looked at Savannah, then his gaze flicked over to Rayne and he smiled but without his usual confidence. "You guys were talking about me?" he said.

Rayne felt a tangle of emotions and knew that whatever he had to talk to her about was not going to be good, so the first emotion she plucked out was anger.

"And Brandon Wallace," she said.

Chase looked thoroughly confused. "Who?"

"The guy you gave my cell phone number to."

"I didn't give your number—" He stopped. "Oh, that guy. He's some friend of my mom's and he said he knew you and planned to donate a bunch of money. I figured you'd want to talk to him. Right?"

"Wrong! You should have asked me first."

"I'm sorry," he said. "He's not some sort of stalker, is he?"

"He's just a regular jerk," Rayne said. "And I was doing fine avoiding him until you gave him my number."

"I am really sorry, Rayne. I didn't know."

She eyed him suspiciously. He was being way too contrite. She'd expected at least a little pissiness in response to her anger. When Rayne didn't say anything else, Savannah looked from her to Chase and back again, and Rayne could see her putting two and two together.

Chase turned to Savannah and said, "Could you give us a minute? I need to talk to Rayne about something."

"Really?" Savannah asked, crossing her arms and looking like she had no plans to go anywhere. Chase glanced at Rayne, the frustration visible in his face.

"It's OK," Rayne said to Savannah.

Savannah looked like she wanted to argue, but then she slowly picked up her wine glass and headed for the stairs. As she passed Chase, she gave him a look that made even Rayne feel chilled. When they heard her bedroom door click shut, Chase turned to Rayne and said, "I wanted to talk to you before you told her."

"I was just getting started, but I think she got the picture," Rayne said.

They were standing only feet apart, and though Rayne ached to touch him, she felt unable to move, taut with nerves. "Why did you want me to wait?"

Chase ran a hand through his already rumpled hair and looked all around the room, everywhere but at her. The silence stretched, and Rayne fought the urge to fill it. He took a deep breath and said, "I finally heard about that Nepal gig."

Her heart beat hard, and her breath caught in her throat.

"When do you leave?" she asked, bracing her hand on the back of the couch to steady herself. It was just a gig, it didn't mean—

"First thing tomorrow."

"Tomorrow?" Her heart was a swirl of emotions and she was still reeling from her encounter with Brandon, but then everything snapped into focus and she saw things with a sudden, unwanted clarity. "You'll miss the gala."

"I'm so sorry," he said, taking a step toward her. Rayne wrapped her arms around herself in a protective stance and took a step back. "It's a great opportunity—"

"Of course it is!" Rayne's voice sounded cold and harsh to her own ears, but she kept going. "And the timing is perfect."

"Perfect? No, it's not."

She'd never felt such intense anger, not even when she found out that Brandon was married. But it was directed mostly at herself. She should have known better. It was her own fault she'd gotten hurt again.

"The timing couldn't be better," she said. "Things were

getting good between us so of course you're taking off. Just like everyone said you would. Just like you did with Crystal. Just like you've done with every woman you've ever dated."

"It's only a couple weeks. A month at the absolute most."

"That's not the point!" Rayne shouted. She wanted to throw something. She wanted to scream until the windows cracked. She never let herself give into emotion like this, except—it suddenly struck her—for the night she and Chase made love. The realization made her want to scream even more. What was it about this man?

"I don't want to break things off," he said, reaching for her arm.

But she twisted away. "Why? So you can make sure you have a warm piece of ass to come back to?" It felt good to say it and even better to see the shocked look on his face.

"Please, Rayne." Chase looked like he was starting to panic, which she thought was surprising because surely he'd been through this before with other women. "I care about you. A lot. I want—"

She was thinking of those other women, of Crystal, when she interrupted him. "I don't care what you want. I'll make it easy for both of us. It's over. Now you can go to Nepal with a clean conscience."

"Rayne, please let me explain," he said with a desperate edge to his voice.

She knew there was sadness just waiting to break through the anger, but she wouldn't let that happen until he was gone. And like a spiteful child, she wanted him to feel some of the pain she did.

"I thought I could be like you," she said. "I thought I could do whatever it was we were doing. Just have fun, be casual and not get emotionally involved—at least not right away. But I can't. And I'm glad I can't. I don't want to be like you. Self-absorbed and alone."

He pulled back as though he'd been slapped. "You think I'm self-absorbed? You think I'm not capable of falling in love?"

"I think you're not capable of feeling anything real because that would be inconvenient. I think you avoid anything that gets in the way of your free-wheeling existence. Anything that makes you accountable to anyone else."

He staggered back a few steps and then looked away from her. She had a moment of regret but told herself it was just an act, one he'd perfected over the years.

"You've been waiting for me to disappoint you from day one," he said, facing her again. "Despite that one incredible night and all the fun we've had together, deep down you've always believed I was the awful guy everyone made me out to be. But you're wrong about me."

She felt a twinge of guilt that he might be right, but she plunged ahead. "Am I? Because coming here to tell me you're leaving the country in less than twenty-four hours and abandoning your commitment to the gala would seem to confirm the rumors."

When he didn't respond, she said in a low voice, "Did you really think I would be OK with you running off at the last minute? Bailing on the fundraiser? Bailing on me?" She was close to tears but fought them back. "After we agreed to start a real relationship after the gala?"

Chase looked away.

"I mean, did you really see this conversation going any other way?" The anger was rapidly leaving Rayne's body and a deep sadness was taking its place. She didn't know how much longer she could do this.

Chase finally looked at her. "I knew you'd be upset, which is why I avoided telling you until now."

She was taken aback. "How long have you known?"

He glanced away again. "Since Sunday."

She closed her eyes, totally out of energy, out of words. Finally she looked up at him, soaking in his beautiful blue eyes and shaggy brown hair one last time. In a clear, calm voice, she said, "Stay in Nepal as long as you like. You've got nothing to rush back to."

He took a step toward her. "Rayne, please," he said. "Please don't do this."

She moved back, out of his reach. "I'd like you to go now."

"I can't leave things like this."

"Get out!" she shouted on the verge of hysterics. "Just go!"

He stumbled back a pace, clearly startled by her tone, but she didn't waver and he finally walked away. She folded her arms tight against her chest because she was shaking from the effort of holding herself together. As soon as the front door closed behind him, she collapsed on the couch and burst into tears.

Savannah flew down the stairs and wrapped Rayne in a fierce hug. As Rayne sobbed onto her shoulder, Savannah stroked her hair and made soothing noises. When her crying subsided, Savannah said in a quiet voice, "How long have you two been seeing each other?"

Rayne pulled away and dug a tissue out of her purse. "A few weeks. Ever since that weekend last month. And please don't say I told you so, even though I totally deserve it."

"I wasn't going to say that," Savannah said. "Why didn't you tell me what was going on?"

Rayne blew her nose. "Because I knew you wouldn't approve. And deep down, I knew it wasn't a good idea." Chase had been right about that—she'd never really trusted him. "We agreed to keep it low key until we could see where it was going and because I wanted to stay focused on the fundraiser. And then once we had the gala, if we were still into each other, we were going to come clean with everyone."

Rayne sat straight up. "Oh, god, the gala! I booked us a room at the Willard. I had this whole romantic thing planned, and now I won't even get to see him in a tux!"

Savannah laughed, and Rayne smiled through her tears.

"I'm really sorry you're hurting, sweetie," Savannah said. "But I do think you dodged a bullet. It's better that you ended it sooner rather than later. And with that stunning dress you just bought, you'll be turning heads at the gala."

"I'm so, so sorry I didn't tell you," Rayne said and started to cry again. "I hated keeping it from you. I don't know why I keep finding these men who can't date me in broad daylight. Like I'm some kind of vampire." It occurred to Rayne that she'd been the one who suggested they keep their relationship a secret. But Chase hadn't tried to talk her out of it, and right now, she was too miserable to make sense of any of it.

Savannah put her arm around her. "They're the vampires. We just need some silver bullets."

"I think that's werewolves," Rayne said with a sniffle. "You kill vampires with a stake through the heart. Or exposure to sunlight."

"Well, I'd say you did a pretty good job of frying our old pal Chase!" Savannah said, then when she saw the look on Rayne's face, added, "Sorry, too soon."

Rayne made an effort to smile. "Yeah, but Brandon must have nuclear-strength sunblock because he's out walking around."

"Ah yes, Brandon. Please tell me you told him to go to hell."

Rayne didn't answer. She was thinking about how handsome he had looked even though, or maybe because, he was so sad and anxious. At least he was capable of emotion.

"Rayney?"

"He told me to call anytime, that it was all up to me. That he wanted me in his life."

"And you said...?"

"Nothing. I didn't know what to say. But I'm not going to call him. I'll let Jeremy take it from here. Speaking of which, Brandon said Jeremy pushed him off the board of directors because of me. Because he figured out what was going on."

"I love that man," Savannah said.

"Get in line!" Rayne said, and they both laughed. "Want to order Chinese takeout and get drunk?"

"I thought you'd never ask!"

Chapter 13

Chase stumbled home from Rayne's house barely aware of where he was or where he was going. The look on her face when he told her about his trip was like a knife through his heart. He'd been prepared for her to be angry, but her voice was so intense, so full of rage that for once he was sorry he'd provoked her passion. And she didn't even give him a chance to explain. She just immediately assumed he was breaking up with her. That hurt, but he shouldn't have been surprised, not when everyone seemed to believe it was their job to warn her off him. And deep down, he'd been afraid of that reaction all along.

It hadn't helped that she'd been angry before he'd even gotten there. About that guy...Brian Walrus—or something? Chase remembered Colin saying some guy really did a number on Rayne and that's why Savannah was so protective. Could Walrus be the guy? And why was he calling her now?

Had Chase just made an even bigger fumble than he realized?

But no, Rayne was angry that Chase had given the guy her number, and why would she be mad if she wanted to hook up with him? Or could she have been trying to cover her feelings?

His mind was still spinning when he got back to his apartment. He looked through his phone's call history, found the guy's number, and googled it. The number belonged to a company in Annapolis that did some kind of management consulting and had some pretty big clients, including government agencies.

Chase went to the website and clicked on "About us" and found the bios of the company's executives. The president and founder was Brandon Wallace.

"Brian Walrus," Chase said under his breath.

Even if the photo wasn't up-to-date—and as a photographer, Chase knew these executive types held onto the best photo they had till well past the time their hair thinned and their cheeks went jowly—the guy had to be a good fifteen years older than Rayne. The bio didn't have much in the way of personal info, so on a hunch, Chase googled "Brandon Wallace" and "wife."

Bingo! He found news items about Brandon and Yvonne Wallace at high-brow events and photos of the man with a beautiful woman who had honey-olive skin and a figure that was made for slinky evening gowns. He could picture her behind one of those old forties microphones singing in a smoky nightclub while all the men fantasized about her.

One of the recent photo captions noted that the couple had been married for ten years. Which meant he had been married when he knew Rayne.

Chase sat back in his chair. So she'd had an affair with a married man. And he'd made a stupid comment about how much he was enjoying sneaking around with her, like he was dating a married woman. And then he'd given this idiot her phone number when she'd clearly been avoiding him—which might or might not mean she still had feelings for him.

Sometimes, Chase thought, I truly am my own worst enemy.

He powered off his laptop and tucked it into his shoulder bag. He had to be at Dulles at an ungodly hour the next morning, so he put his bags by the front door and headed out to Zipped to face Colin's wrath. He assumed Colin would have heard from Savannah by now, and he was hoping he could get some brotherly advice because despite what Rayne thought, he wasn't ready to end their relationship.

As Chase settled himself at the bar, Colin greeted him warmly and poured him a glass of Sam Adams beer, and Chase realized that Savannah hadn't called yet. He briefly wondered if that was because she was busy comforting Rayne, but he hated to think about Rayne crying, so he took a long sip of beer and said, "Hey, bro, I need to talk to you about something."

"Give me a few minutes, and I'll be back over," Colin said,

dumping a tower of dirty glasses into a rubber bin behind the bar.

"Actually, I wanted to talk to you before you hear it from Savannah, so..."

Colin stared at Chase for a second then tossed down the white towel he'd just picked up. Bracing his arms on the bar, he gave Chase his full, if slightly wary, attention. "OK, what's up?" he said. And then his cell phone rang.

Colin pulled it out of his pocket and smiled as he held it up to show Chase Savannah's name on the screen. "Too late."

"Don't answer it!" Chase said.

Colin looked at him like he was insane and hit the answer button.

"Hey, sweetie," he said into the phone. A second later, he glanced at Chase. "Yeah, he just got here."

Chase squirmed in his seat, feeling a sudden urge to grab the phone and smash it.

"Did he now?" Colin said, and Chase didn't know if Savannah was telling him about Rayne or Nepal.

"Tomorrow, eh? Well, I hear Nepal is pretty nice this time of year," Colin said, shaking his head at Chase. "I can get rid of him if you two want to come here for dinner. And by dinner I mean liquor."

Chase put his head in his hands.

After listening for a few minutes, Colin said, "OK, I understand. I'll check in on you later, but let me know if I can do anything. And tell Rayne I'm sorry."

As Colin set the phone down, he let out a long whistle. "Wow. This is low even for you."

Chase lifted his head. "Christ almighty," he said before his brother could launch into a full tirade. "I can never get a word in edgewise around here. Just once I'd like to be able to explain myself before everyone assumes I'm a selfish asshole."

"Fine. Explain," Colin said coldly.

Chase opened his mouth but suddenly didn't know where to begin.

"Dude, today," Colin said, slapping the bar.

Chase was starting to think his sister Jessica would have been a better source of sympathy. "I like her. I really do. A lot."

Colin raised an eyebrow and waited.

"I screwed up, OK? I know that. I've been trying to get this gig in Nepal since before she and I hooked up. And it just came through a few days ago and I didn't know how to tell her so I waited till the last minute."

Colin was still eyeing him coldly. "And it never occurred to you to say no this one time?"

"How could I? I've been working this contact for weeks. If I said no now, I'd look like a joke and he'd never work with me again, and that sort of thing gets around." Chase ran a hand through his hair. "And I have to be there on Thursday because that's when the writer is there. I tried to explain, but after everything you and Savannah have told her about me, she just assumed—"

"Don't you put this on me!" Colin said. "This is entirely your doing. You could have at least waited a few days so you wouldn't be missing the gala."

Chase was silent for a moment. "It never even occurred to me. When the guy told me the writer would be there in three days, I just automatically said I could, too. I didn't even stop to think about it."

"God, you're hopeless!" Colin threw his arms up and walked away.

Chase definitely should have gone to Jessica for comfort. When Diana walked up to ask what he wanted to eat, he said he wasn't hungry. He drained his beer then pushed himself away from the bar and went looking for Colin. He found him in his office.

"I need a favor," Chase said, his hand on the doorframe as though he needed the support to stay upright.

"Really? What a surprise," Colin said, dropping his pen and leaning back in his chair.

"Why are you acting like I stole your Matchbox cars?" Chase asked, his patience nearly worn away. "What does this even have to do with you?"

"Oh, I don't know," Colin said. "Maybe because if Rayne is upset, Savannah is upset, and if Savannah is upset, it has to do with me. Which is exactly why I told you to stay away from Rayne."

Chase could feel a migraine building behind his eyes. Stupid, complicated life. Suddenly Nepal didn't feel far enough away.

Rubbing his eyes, he said, "Look, I just need you to keep an eye on her—especially at the gala. There's this guy... Brian. Brandon, maybe? I'm not really sure what the story is, but I think he might be the guy Savannah told you about, the one who really did a number on her. He's been calling her." Chase left out the part about him giving the guy her number.

"And you want me to do what exactly?" Colin asked. "Keep your ex-girlfriend from hooking up with anyone else while you're gallivanting around Asia?"

"Just keep an eye on her, please. Don't let him get close to her. I'll fix everything when I get back."

"Famous last words," Colin said. But when Chase kept staring at him, he finally said, "OK, fine. I'll do what I can. But I wouldn't get my hopes up if I were you."

Chase went to bed early, but he couldn't sleep. He just lay there in the dark going over things in his head. Around midnight, he started to text Rayne but kept erasing and starting over and finally realized that what he needed to say wouldn't fit in a text. And it was too late to call her.

If he wasn't leaving town, he could treat it like a fight, give her some time to calm down, and then they'd make up and have mind-blowing sex. But if he wasn't leaving, they wouldn't have even fought in the first place. It made his head hurt, and he finally reached the point where he was so exhausted that he told himself he'd figure it out in Nepal. Everything was always easier once he got on a plane.

He'd barely fallen asleep when his alarm went off at 4 a.m. He felt weirdly hung over as he stumbled to the shower. He hadn't left himself much time to get ready before the airport shuttle was due to arrive, and the fact that he was moving in slow motion didn't help. He barely had enough time to shower, dress, throw his toiletries in his bag, wolf down a bowl of cereal, and lug his gear downstairs.

Riding in the van toward the suburbs, he watched the first rays of sunrise color the early morning gloom as sleepy commuters headed the other direction into the city. Slowly, he started to feel his usual excitement. He had everything he needed right there with him, and he felt free. He told himself it was good that he'd taken the gig because if Rayne couldn't understand that about him—couldn't appreciate the core of him—then it never would have lasted anyway. There would have been another overseas gig or another ex-boyfriend with money and status who would have come between them. He wished he could have stayed for the gala, but it couldn't be helped.

Instead of being vindicated, though, he was sadder than he could ever remember feeling.

At the airport, he checked in for his flight and wound his way through security, then rode the people mover to the terminal, where he bought coffee and a danish and sat down to wait for his flight. The writer he'd be working with was already in New Delhi, and they planned to meet up in Kathmandu that night— which would actually be the next day because of the long flight and eleven-hour time difference.

Chase picked up a newspaper that another traveler had abandoned and scanned the news. Tensions in Kashmir between India and Pakistan. Protests in Delhi over a string of assaults on women, a sea change in the making. Unrest along the border between China and Mongolia. Lots of promising opportunities for a photojournalist. He was starting to warm up to the idea of staying in that part of the world for a while after this assignment ended. He'd never been to China, had always wanted to see Mongolia.

As he was waiting in line to board the plane, he got an email from an artist he'd contacted who'd been out of town for the past few weeks. He wanted to donate a painting for the fundraiser. Chase was almost at the gate, so he quickly forwarded the message to Rayne's personal email account, cc:'ing the artist, so he couldn't say much, just Good luck with the event.

He didn't expect a response. And he didn't get one.

Chapter 14

After her blowup with Chase, Rayne barely touched her General Tso's chicken and drank way too much wine. She slept fitfully and missed her alarm the next morning, and when she woke up, her first thought was of Chase getting on a plane. Her second thought was the realization that her throbbing head and nausea meant she had a migraine.

She dragged herself out of bed and glanced at her phone. She had an email from Chase about another painting for the gala. Her eyes filled with tears, and she shoved the phone deep into her purse and headed for the shower.

When she got to work, she walked straight into Sheila's office with her sunglasses still on and handed her Brandon's business card. Sheila looked at the card and back at Rayne. "What's this for?" she asked.

"Brandon got Vincent to drop the sale price by five percent, and he'll match whatever we raise at the gala," Rayne said. "Tell Jeremy to get in touch with him."

"Oh my god, that's incredible!" Sheila said. "He just cut our fundraising needs in half. Even more than that. I can't wait to tell Jeremy. But how did you... how did he...?" She took a closer look at Rayne. "Are you feeling OK?"

"Migraine," Rayne said. "Is the coffee machine fixed?"

Sheila nodded. "But maybe you should go home instead. We can cover things here."

Rayne shook her head. The gala was only three days away. "I'm fine. A little caffeine should do the trick."

She turned to go and saw a large framed photo of the very house she was standing in and recognized it as one that Chase had taken. Beside it was a series of photographs of the Borneo rainforest.

"He dropped those off yesterday afternoon," Sheila said. "There are five in all. Very generous of him. He does beautiful work."

"Yeah," Rayne said.

"Did he catch up with you yesterday? He was looking for you, seemed pretty anxious to find you."

"He found me." She wanted to blame it on the migraine— they always made her weepy—but she knew that wasn't why she had tears in her eyes. And she was grateful for the sunglasses. She just might keep them on all day.

Chase slept most of the way to Kathmandu. Over the years, he'd developed a knack for sleeping whenever and wherever he could. Often enough he had to be awake when he really needed to sleep so he'd gotten used to getting by on a few hours here and there when he was on assignment. It could be a little surreal. Sometimes he wasn't sure when he was awake and when he was dreaming, especially when he got on a plane in an orderly airport like Dulles and landed in the mayhem of a third-world country.

Kathmandu's airport was full of young hippie wannabees, white kids with Rasta dreadlocks and heavy, Army surplus backpacks looking—and smelling—like they'd been traveling for weeks. Mingling among them were the serious hikers, who had likely come to trek the Himalayas or maybe hike to base camp on Everest (no one tried to summit the mountain this time of year). Chase shared an affinity with those guys, not the ones who paid tens of thousands of dollars for someone to basically lead them up the mountain so they could say they'd done it but the guys who came back more than once, driven by the challenge and the opportunity to test the limits of their self-reliance.

He was feeling the effects of his jumbled sleep and the altitude—had to get his sea legs back—so he went straight to the guest house he'd booked online.

On the taxi ride over, Chase was surprised and saddened to see that the earthquake's destruction looked fresh even though it had happened several months ago. The rubble had been cleared away for the most part, but buildings still showed gaping wounds or sat roofless and exposed to the elements, sometimes with people living in the ruins. Conspiculously missing from the skyline was the tall white Dharahara Tower, which had crumbled to the ground. He trudged into the guest house feeling drained, but he brightened when he saw the young woman behind the counter. "Namaste," he said.

She had the smooth brown skin, high cheekbones, and wide smile of a native Nepali. Long silky black hair and a slender figure, too. Her name came to him instantly: Maya. Funny, he probably never would have remembered if he'd met her in the States.

"Namaste!" she said with a smile. "It's good to see you again, Chase Allison."

"It's good to see you, too, Sunshine. Any way I can get the room in the front corner again?"

"It's all ready for you." She handed him a key.

"Thanks. Oh, and I'm meeting up with someone this evening—a writer named Roy Fellows. If I'm not downstairs by then, could someone come and wake me up?"

"It would be my pleasure," she said, still smiling that dazzling smile.

He shook his head, grinning. She had to be seventeen at most. "You are a dangerous woman. But still much too young for me."

"Getting older every minute," she said as he headed for the stairs.

Settling into his room, he realized that he hadn't thought about Rayne since falling asleep on the plane. Well, that wasn't exactly true. She was always hovering in the back of his mind, but he hadn't obsessed about how they'd left things in hours, and it was a relief. Once again, everything was easier when he was traveling.

Once Rayne had a cup of coffee and got down to work, she started to feel better, more in control. When Colin stopped by to finalize the catering plan, they wandered around the house together deciding where they'd put tables and chairs for maximum traffic through the house.

"I think your best bet is having a couple waiters moving around with trays of food, and also small stations of food and a bar on each floor, plus the foyer," Colin said. "That way no one has to go far from the art to get food or drinks."

"Yes, absolutely," Rayne said.

Colin confirmed that they would be having finger foods, including artichoke turnovers, pancetta-wrapped figs, and mini-crab cakes—along with champagne and a few types of wine.

As she walked him to the front door, he said, "This is a beautiful old house. I can see why you want to save it."

"Thank you so much for helping out," she said.

He paused in the foyer and faced her. "I just want to say that Chase is an ass, and I'm really sorry."

Rayne felt tears start behind her eyes—migraine and fatigue, of course—and forced herself to smile. "I appreciate it."

"If you're looking for a date to the gala, I know a lot of guys who are much more reliable than my brother. I'd be happy to set something up."

"God, no! I mean, I'm fine. And I'll be so busy I wouldn't be able to keep track of a date anyway. But thanks." The truth was that the thought of being there with anyone other than Chase was too much to contemplate.

"No problem."

He reached for the door, and she put a hand on his arm. "I'm so happy you and Savannah are together. I was rooting for you the whole time, you know. And what happened between Chase and me doesn't have to affect our friendship."

He smiled. "Absolutely not. I'll see you Saturday."

He gave her a quick kiss on the cheek, and she felt better, she felt connected, and in a spiteful moment, she hoped that Chase was feeling lonely.

Colin headed down the front steps, then ran back up to hold the door for Crystal, who was carrying two large paintings wrapped in brown paper. She came inside breathless and red-faced from the exertion.

"I brought two," she said. "I hope that's still OK."

"Absolutely!" Rayne said. "Put them over here." She gestured to Crystal to lean the paintings against the stairway. "Can I take a peek?"

Crystal undid the masking tape and started to pull the paper away. Rayne caught flashes of brilliant turquoise, red, and green and something that looked like a long swooping tail.

"They're a little abstract, but this one is a quetzal bird and the other is a great green macaw," Crystal said. "Both birds are in trouble in the wild."

"Gorgeous!" Rayne said, then realized her co-worker Kyle had come up behind her and was staring at the paintings. Then he glanced shyly at Crystal.

"Hey, Kyle, meet Crystal, one of our artists," Rayne said, stepping back to let Kyle get a better view of the paintings.

Kyle was CACC's entire IT department, and he'd been working on an app that would make it easier for people to bid on the paintings at the gala or if they couldn't attend in person. He always seemed to be wearing nice jeans and a button-down shirt with the sleeves rolled up. He had an adorable baby face and was the sort of guy she pictured taking computers apart in his spare time, just for fun. Rayne didn't know him all that well because he tended to keep to himself. But he was pleasant and friendly when she did interact with him, and she had yet to hear of an IT problem he couldn't solve.

"Crystal, meet Kyle, our IT guy. He's been working on an app that will let people bid on the paintings using their smart phones."

"Oh wow, that's so cool! Great to meet you!" Crystal said, holding out her hand to Kyle.

"Your paintings are beautiful," Kyle said as he took her hand. "Not that I know anything about art."

Crystal laughed. "You don't need to know anything about art to say whether you like a painting or not. And thanks."

"Listen, I need to get back to work," Rayne said. "Sheila's right inside that room over there, and she's got some paperwork for you to fill out. Maybe Kyle can help you take the paintings into her office."

Kyle looked a little flustered. "I need to talk to you about the app," he said, pointing to the cell phone in his hand. "I had an idea about how to get all the paintings scanned in so people can bid even if they aren't on site Saturday night."

"That's fantastic. Come up in about ten minutes and we'll talk about it," Rayne said then turned back to Crystal. "We're all set on the desserts for Saturday, right?"

"Yes! Dozens of mini cupcakes and fruit tarts will be here that afternoon."

Seeing the confused look on Kyle's face, Crystal laughed and put her hand on his arm. "I'm a baker by trade—for now, at least—but art is my passion." Then with another big smile, she turned to pick up a painting and headed toward Sheila's office. Without a word, Kyle picked up the other one and followed her.

Rayne went upstairs and sat down behind her desk. She was feeling a little shaky and wanted to catch her breath. Between the blow-up with Chase, getting very little sleep, and the coffee she'd drunk to counteract the migraine, she was jittery. She turned the chair so she could see out the back window and was lost in thought when Jeremy knocked on the open door and walked in.

She was embarrassed to be caught doing nothing. "Sorry, just taking a breather before I meet with Kyle about the app."

"I didn't come here to check up on you." He had his hand on the door as though he couldn't make up his mind about closing it. Her heart, which was already unsteady, started beating hard.

He finally sat down in the chair on the other side of the desk with the door still ajar. "Sheila told me about Brandon Wallace's offer. That's very generous of him."

"I thought so, too."

He paused. "I'm more than a little surprised to hear from him though," he finally said.

"Me, too." She was feeling so awkward that she prayed Kyle would burst in now.

He glanced away from her, and she suddenly realized that he was as uncomfortable as she was. She had a brief fantasy of him saying, "Steer clear of Brandon so you can be with me." That would show Chase, she thought and immediately felt silly. She really needed to stay away from coffee on days like this.

"I'm friends with Yvonne—his wife," Jeremy said. "She moved out about a month ago. Which made me wonder about the timing of his offer."

So Brandon hadn't lied—at least, not about his wife leaving. But there was another question behind Jeremy's statement.

"He got an invitation from Bea Allison," she said, answering the obvious question.

"Ah, I see. Well, he would have been on our mailing list anyway."

She knew he was trying to broach the subject of her and Brandon, but she wasn't about to help him. Where the hell was Kyle?

Jeremy leaned forward. "I'm probably overstepping, but I wanted to say that I feel like I let you down a year ago. I could see how he looked at you, and he never wore his wedding ring so I wasn't sure what exactly was going on—and I don't need to know the details—but I should have talked to you then. And I should have kicked his ass off the board the minute I even suspected."

Rayne laughed. God, it felt good to laugh. It felt even better to know how protective Jeremy was of her.

"I've never heard you swear before," she said.

He smiled. "I'm glad you're feeling better. Sheila's worried about you. She said you looked like you'd been carrying water for the devil all night—her expression."

It was nice to have so many people looking out for her, though if they kept warning her off men, she'd never be able to date again.

"I'm fine," she said. "But I will let you deal with Brandon."

"Good." He stood up to go. "Oh, and let me know when you and Chase are planning to hang all the artwork. I'd be happy to help. I feel like I've barely done anything compared to all the hard work you two have done."

Rayne's smile faded, and she suddenly took a keen interest in the stack of papers on her desk. "Actually, he just left for a photo assignment in Nepal. He won't be coming to the gala. But Sheila and I can handle the artwork."

Jeremy frowned. "I'm surprised to hear that. I just assumed he'd be around for the event."

You're not the only one, she thought bitterly.

Kyle walked into the office before he realized Rayne wasn't alone.

"Oh, sorry, I'll come back—"

Jeremy waved a hand. "No worries. I was just leaving." To Rayne, he said, "How about first thing Saturday for hanging the artwork? I can bring some tools. And maybe Kyle here can help out."

Kyle looked a little flustered, but he nodded. "I can do that."

"And let me know if you need help with anything else in Chase's absence," Jeremy said.

"Sure thing," Rayne said and resisted the urge to ask if he could fix a broken heart.

Chase slept more soundly than he'd expected, especially with the window open and the rumble of diesel engines and the constant clamor of people talking on the street below. He'd forgotten about the pollution in Kathmandu, the pall that often hung over the town and irritated the throat and lungs and stung the eyes.

But he wouldn't be staying more than a couple days. He and Roy would soon take off for the villages. Chase was looking forward to the rugged outdoors.

When he woke up, the sky was already turning to twilight and streetlights were coming on. He looked at his watch, but he'd forgotten to set it to local time and there was no clock in his room. He washed his face and brushed his teeth and went downstairs to meet up with Roy.

Maya wasn't behind the counter, but her mother was. She greeted Chase warmly.

"What time is it?" he asked, watch in hand.

"Nearly 7:00."

He glanced up at her. "Could you be a little more specific?"

She laughed. "You Americans and your fancy watches." She consulted a clock on the counter and said, "6:47."

He set his watch and then checked his phone. No message from Roy, even though they'd agreed to meet at 6:30.

"Has anyone left a message for me?" he asked, but she said no.

So he sat down in a chair by the door and waited. He flipped through the travel brochures and spent some time reading the one about a bus tour to Chitwan National Park. Around 7:30, he finally got an email from Roy: *Stuck in Delhi. Will be in Kath day after tomorrow.*

Chase sent a short message back saying he'd see him in two days. Then he stuck the brochure in his pocket and wandered outside to find something to eat. The trip to Chitwan was about five hours by bus. He could leave in the morning, spend the day taking photos of the wildlife, crash at a cheap hotel, and return to Kathmandu by the time Roy hit town. That's the beauty of traveling alone, he thought. You can change plans on a dime and you don't have to negotiate with anyone else.

After a dinner of vegetable-stuffed dumplings and a pot of smoky Darjeeling tea, he went back to his room and put his camera and a few essentials in his shoulder bag. But he couldn't find his antimalarial pills, which he technically should have started taking before he even left D.C. He dumped the contents of his suitcase out on the bed and pawed through everything, but they weren't there. He closed his eyes and tried to picture himself packing—and he could clearly see the medicine sitting on his nightstand.

"Shit," he said out loud.

He'd had malaria once before, a couple years ago, but it hadn't hit him until he'd gotten back to D.C. Colin had taken him to the doctor right away so Chase had only muddled through a few days of body-rattling chills and vomiting before the meds kicked in. The disease was rampant—and deadly—in many parts of the world, and though Kathmandu was relatively safe, once he ventured away from the city, he'd be vulnerable. It was the tail end of monsoon season, so it wasn't peak malaria time, but the mosquitoes that carried the disease might still be active.

"Goddamn idiot," he said, running a hand through his hair in exasperation.

If he hadn't been thinking about Rayne, he would have done his traditional final sweep of the room and seen the medicine. Maybe he could borrow some bug spray from someone on the bus. But that stuff only lasted a couple hours, and in Chase's experience, nothing totally protected you from bugs. They seemed to be getting tougher and more aggressive, and he briefly wondered if climate change had anything to do with it. But that was Rayne's domain, and he wasn't thinking about her now. At least, not if he could help it.

He decided he'd go on the bus trip anyway because he didn't want to just hang around in Kathmandu until Roy got there. He'd be careful, and as soon as he got back to town, he'd find a doctor who could give him the pills.

He got into bed and tossed and turned for a long time. It wasn't like him to forget something like that. It made him realize that he'd lost his head a little over Rayne. He'd been so worried about upsetting her that he hadn't had his mind properly focused on his trip.

That shit ends now, he decided.

Chapter 15

When Chase got off the bus in Chitwan, he was swarmed by locals wanting to offer him a ride, a tour of the park, and god knows what else. But he shrugged them off with a smile and headed down the road for the fifteen-minute walk to the park. He had a slight headache, and it felt good to walk. Plus, he could stop along the way and snap photos of the goats and stray dogs and children darting about.

Once at the park, he approached one of the drivers of a jeep tour who wasn't much older than him and had an easy smile. Chase figured they'd get along well. He explained that he was a professional photographer and he'd like a private tour. He haggled with the guy—who introduced himself as Tenzin—for a while until they agreed on a price. Chase climbed into the jeep, and they took off into the park.

It was like entering another world. The park was miles of grasslands and forest, and the animals looked right at home. He saw single-horned rhinos, sloth bears, and golden jackals as readily as he would see pigeons or squirrels in D.C. He was grateful that the days of having to load rolls of film were gone. He took so many photos, though, that he had to switch out the memory card for a new one.

At one stop, Tenzin waved his hat in front of his face to chase away the bugs and said, "You're lucky. It's the first day we've had no rain in a week."

"Oh? Isn't it late a little late for the rainy season?" Chase asked as he lined up a shot of an antelope herd in the grass up ahead.

"It seems to start earlier and last longer every year," Tenzin said. "But then it's so hot and dry in the summer it's like it never rained."

Chase took a series of photos then turned to look at him. "Climate change, do you think?"

Tenzin nodded. "Something is changing. During the monsoons, my village has landslides and floods like we've have never seen before."

Even in Nepal, he couldn't get away from Rayne. The photos he was taking would be perfectly suited to the gala. Maybe the organization could use them some other way. He thought about sending her a couple of the shots, but that seemed like pouring salt in the wound. Like a postcard that says: *Having a great time without you. Glad I'm here.*

"And the glaciers," Tenzin said, putting his hat back on. "If you go trekking up in the Himalayas, you'll see what I mean. They're shrinking. Drying up."

"I'm sorry to hear that," Chase said. Trekking in the Himalayas was an interesting idea, though. More photos, more time away from D.C.

They stayed out until dusk, and Tenzin dropped him at a restaurant in town. Chase drank a beer and ate a delicious bowl of rice and lentils then went in search of a cheap room, which he found at the edge of town. He drifted off to sleep to the sound of snoring on the other side of the thin wall. Ah, the romance of foreign travel, he thought.

The morning of the gala, Rayne walked into the office at 7 a.m. after another restless night, wearing jeans and a T-shirt. She was carrying a makeup case and her new dress in a garment bag. Sheila was already there, dressed like Rayne but still managing to look stylish. She had her hair pulled back in a ponytail and was ready for business.

With Kyle's help, they had spent the afternoon and evening before photographing all the images and making color printouts. Now they spread the printouts on the floor at the foot of the stairs and grouped the images together by subject matter, color, and framing style and rearranged them into different combinations.

When they were satisfied, they lightly taped the images on

the walls of the entryway, dining room (which served as their conference room), hallways, and various offices. Jeremy showed up at 10 with a couple hammers and a picture-hanging kit. As he walked around and looked at the images tacked to the walls, Rayne took in his casual dress of jeans, sneakers, and a University of Virginia T-shirt. She'd never seen him so casual, and she had to admit it was a good look for him.

He suggested some changes to the order of the artwork, specifically the fact that Rayne had put Chase's photos in a dark corner beside the stairs—except for the one of the house itself, which Sheila had placed beside her office door where everyone would see it when they walked in.

"I think these would do better over here," Jeremy said, taking the printouts of Chase's Borneo photos and moving them to the opposite wall, next to the photo of the house. The location was bigger and brighter, but now Rayne would have to see the images and think of Chase every time she walked through.

"Don't you think?" Jeremy said, looking at her over his shoulder.

"Yes, of course," Rayne said.

"I might just have to buy a couple of these myself," Jeremy said. And Rayne prayed he'd hang them at home and not in his office.

Kyle showed up just before lunchtime, excited to show them the page he'd created on their website with the scans of all the artwork and directions for how to bid using the app. Rayne rushed to her office to send the link out over their social media accounts and email list. Then they ordered pizza and ate as they hung the artwork and handled other last-minute tasks. Rayne was starting to feel a little less down. She was grateful she wasn't alone. Whenever her gaze fell on Chase's photos, she quickly looked at Sheila and Kyle and Jeremy talking or arguing or laughing and felt happy to be part of something so special. And pitied Chase for holding himself apart from it.

Chase woke up the next morning with the same headache and a soreness in his limbs that he blamed on the bouncy jeep ride.

He had some tea and toast at the hotel and then headed outside, where Tenzin was already waiting to take him back to the park until it was time for Chase to catch the bus to Kathmandu.

His headache started to clear as soon as he began taking photos. Or maybe he just didn't notice it anymore. They roamed around the park for hours, sharing Tenzin's thermos of tea and snacking on Chase's stash of chocolate and power bars. It was afternoon when Tenzin dropped him off near the bus stop. Chase got out of the jeep and handed him a generous tip.

"Thanks, man," he said. "I really appreciate the private tour. Namaste."

Tenzin smiled, bowed his head slightly, and sped off.

Chase was feeling fine at that moment. And then he walked across the road to the bus stop and everything changed.

It came on suddenly, like the flu, but it felt like something much worse. For once, he was thinking that his cavalier attitude toward sleep might be his undoing. That and all the stress before he left town could be enough to make him sick.

He hadn't been bitten by a mosquito, he was sure of it, and besides, it took at least a week for symptoms of malaria to show up. It could be a relapse from his earlier bout. Was that better or worse than getting the disease again?

He was one of the first people in line for the bus, and he headed straight for the back where he could be near the toilet. He put his bag on the seat next to him and hunkered down, hoping other people would assume he was traveling with someone and move on.

"Hey, buddy, you don't look so good." Chase opened his eyes to see a tall, beefy Texan in a polo shirt with a camera slung around his neck. "It's nothing contagious, is it?"

Chase tried to smile, but his teeth were chattering. "Just a cold," he said. Colds were contagious but not deadly, and maybe it would be enough to convince the guy to find another seat.

"Buddy, that ain't no cold," the Texan said.

Stop calling me buddy, Chase thought irritably. He just wanted to get back to Kathmandu where he'd have a better shot at finding a doctor. He didn't want to be stranded out here in

Chitwan. If he could get some medicine, he might be able to sleep it off in a day or two and still hook up with Roy for the assignment.

The Texan eyed him for a minute then squeezed into the seat across the aisle, next to a plump young woman with a huge backpack in her lap. Chase leaned his head against the window and closed his eyes. Five hours back to Kathmandu. Could he keep from vomiting for five hours?

He couldn't. Before the bus even hit the main road, he had to dive into the bathroom. He vomited so hard and so long that there was nothing left in his system. His stomach ached from the effort. He splashed water on his face and stumbled back to his seat. He was shivering from the chills, and he had a blinding headache. Every bump in the road was pure torture.

Chase took a sip of water from his bottle as the Texan watched him from across the aisle. He tried to distract himself by thinking about what day it was back in D.C. Late afternoon in Nepal was the wee hours of the morning in D.C. It was Saturday. The gala was tonight. But Rayne's tonight, not his. He made a mental note to send her a text first thing tomorrow morning, when she'd be getting ready for the gala. Probably putting on an evening gown.

The bus hit a pothole and bounced. Chase's stomach clenched, and his head felt like an elephant was standing on it. *What color?* he asked himself. *What color is Rayne's dress? Black? Red? Snug or slinky?*

It wasn't working. He still felt sick and now he was missing Rayne.

And then it hit him. He was alone in a foreign country, dangerously ill and about to slip into delirium, and everyone who cared about him was halfway across the world and half a day behind him. He'd never felt so low.

He gripped his camera bag to his chest, suddenly aware of how easy it would be for someone to rob him. How long had he been on the bus? He looked out the window, but he was having trouble focusing. It was getting dark out, and the people in the bus were reflected back at him in the glass. But their faces looked ghastly and skeletal. When the lights of cars streamed past, the streaks hurt his eyes. Rain drummed on the roof of the bus, and he felt the hammering in his bones. The bus splashed through huge puddles, the windows were streaked with water, and he felt like he was drowning.

He looked at his watch but couldn't make out the time in the dim light and couldn't remember how to make the dial light up. Then he began to wonder if he was awake or asleep. He could feel the bus moving so either way, he was getting closer to Kathmandu. He wanted to stay awake, he thought that would be safer, but he was aware of slipping away.

It was raining. Rayning. Everywhere. He saw her face in the window. She was wearing a yellow slicker and a silly matching hat with a brim and a chin strap. He laughed. But she didn't laugh. She had that look on her face, the same one she'd had when he told her he was going to Nepal. Like an arrow through the heart. But not the good kind. Not the cupid kind. She was holding a bird with a white head and brown wings and then he saw the feet and recognized the blue-footed booby, the bird on her cell phone, and Chase wished he could hit rewind and go back to that night when she'd left her phone at Zipped and start over.

He must have been talking to himself because a man with a Texas accent said, "What's that, buddy?"

"Nothing," Chase mumbled. I'm on a bus, he reminded himself. In Texas. No, Nepal. The Texan was sitting across the aisle. Chase lay curled up on the seat, his arms still hugging the camera bag.

"Where are you staying?" the man asked.

Stay—why hadn't she asked him to stay? Because she knew he'd say no? "I never should have left," Chase said, feeling miserable.

"Well, you gotta leave now because the bus has stopped. We're in Kathmandu."

Chase struggled to sit upright and gazed around. The bus had indeed stopped moving, and the last of the passengers were filing out into the night. Everything was a swirl of light and color and water.

"Kathmandu?" he said uncertainly.

"Do you have a place to stay?" the man asked, sounding impatient now.

Chase told him the name and address of the guest house and was proud of himself for remembering. He got to his feet, which was awkward because he was still clutching his bag to his chest. The man reached out a hand to help him, but Chase said, "I'm fine."

"You are far from fine, but suit yourself," the man said. "At least let me get you into a cab."

Chase couldn't remember ever feeling so suspicious or paranoid. But as soon as he started to walk, he realized that he was going to need the help. He wove down the aisle with one hand on his bag and the other grabbing the back of each seat in turn with the man holding onto his elbow the whole way.

He got down the steps all right but nearly collapsed when his feet hit the road.

"Steady there, buddy," the Texan said. He guided Chase to a nearby taxi and opened the back door. As Chase climbed inside, the Texan gave the driver the name and address of the guest house. To Chase, he said, "I'm assuming you've got money."

Chase nodded and said, "Thanks."

"Just looking out for a fellow American," the man said and swung the door shut.

Chase fought the urge to lie down across the backseat of the cab and struggled to keep his eyes open for the short drive to the guest house. Every muscle in his body ached, and even though there was nothing left in his stomach, he was so nauseated he was sure he would vomit.

The taxi pulled up in front of the guest house, and Chase handed the driver a wad of money that must have been enough or even too much because the guy let him stumble out of the cab. He walked slowly inside. Everything was wobbly, the whole world was swaying. It was Saturday night, and the front room was crowded with lots of people coming and going. He glanced behind the counter and saw that Maya was working, but she didn't see him. He made his way to the stairs and slowly, painfully climbed up to his room.

When he got there, he shut the door, stripped down to his underwear, crawled into bed, and finally let himself go to sleep.

In the middle of the night, he woke up enough to stumble down the hall to the bathroom. He found an unopened bottle of water in his duffel bag and drank half of it. Then he remembered his mental note and sent Rayne a text message saying *Good luck tonight* and closed his eyes and went back to sleep. Or tried to anyway. Between the chills and the sweats, he kept waking up, and when he did fall asleep, he dreamed about being stranded—on islands in the middle of the ocean, on buses plunging off cliffs, high up a mountain with no way down.

And he dreamed about her. At first she was alone, but then he started seeing her with that guy, Brian Walrus. They were in a nightclub and Rayne was wearing an evening gown and bright red lipstick and the guy was kissing her and she was saying *I wouldn't chase him. I never chased him. He ran away.*

Thank god you're here.

Chapter 16

When all the paintings and photographs were up, the four of them took a few moments to admire their work. Then Kyle and Jeremy left, and Rayne and Sheila spent the next couple of hours wrapping small white Christmas lights down the length of the stair railing and around the windows and doorways. As Colin's staff started to arrive to set up the tables and food stations, Rayne arranged candles and pumpkins of all sizes and fresh evergreen sprigs on mantels and windowsills, reveling in the activity and energy swirling through the old house.

Around 5, she went upstairs to change in her private bathroom. She slipped on the dress and shimmery sheer pantyhose and stood there in stockinged feet applying her makeup. She went a little more dramatic than usual—gray eye shadow to complement her eyes, a swoop of eyeliner, and lots of mascara. She brushed on some blush and was putting on a pair of sparkly dangling earrings when her phone beeped. She dug it out of her purse and saw that it was a text message—from Chase.

Her heart betrayed her by giving a little leap. The message was short, but it took her a moment to puzzle it out: *Ghood luckt ongith.* Chase's messages were usually spelled right, and if it hadn't been so timely, she would have guessed he'd texted her by accident by sitting on his phone.

She thought about sending him a quick *Thanks!* Or a *Screw you.* But in the end, she just put the phone back in her purse and slipped on her shoes. She walked out of the bathroom and smoothed down the front of her dress, wishing she had a full-length mirror to check her appearance in. She reached the foot of the stairs just as Sheila was holding the front door open for

Colin. He let out a wolf whistle when he saw Rayne.

"Thanks—I needed that!" she said.

"Totally deserved. You look beautiful."

Sheila excused herself, and Rayne turned her attention to helping Colin and his sister Jessica get the food into the kitchen, where they would finish the prep work and keep the wine and champagne chilled. The wait staff started to arrive, and everything was bustling.

Sheila reappeared in a beaded dress of pale gold that looked straight out of the 1920s.

"You look sensational!" Rayne said. "I knew you would. Are you bringing a date?"

Sheila smiled. "Nope. I thought I'd see if I could cozy up to a wealthy bachelor tonight."

Just then, Jeremy walked through the door in a tux with a brocade cummerbund and matching tie.

"That's where I'd start getting cozy," Rayne said in a low voice.

Sheila sighed. "I try to pretend he's my brother. I like working here too much to take a chance on wrecking my job."

"It's a mystery to me why some woman hasn't snatched him up by now," Rayne said.

"He goes on plenty of dates, but he never seems to get serious. He's too wrapped up in running this organization, if you ask me."

"Or he hasn't found the right woman yet," Rayne said, and they both sighed.

Jeremy walked over to them. "The place looks outstanding," he said. "You two have done an incredible job. I'm thinking you could moonlight as interior decorators."

They both smiled, enjoying the praise.

"Anything I can do?" he asked. "Or is it safe to assume you've got everything under control?"

"Actually, I need you to sign off on the catering order," Sheila said and then led him into the kitchen.

With just an hour to go before the guests started arriving, Rayne did a last-minute sweep of all the rooms, straightening a painting or two, making sure Colin had what he needed. She'd asked Kyle to set up a small sound system—just a couple of speakers connected to a laptop loaded with classical music and jazz—and now she turned the music on low and strategically dimmed some of the overhead lights. Then the guests started to arrive, and she and Sheila were busy greeting people and explaining the bidding process and pointing out the refreshments.

Half an hour later, Savannah walked in the door and stopped. "Oh, it's just beautiful! Like a fairy tale!" She gave Rayne a big hug.

"I'm so glad you're here," Rayne said, holding on tight.

"I wouldn't miss it for the world. Besides, it gives me an excuse to wear this dress again," Savannah said with a smile as she ran her hand down the sexy blue dress she'd bought her for the gala she'd thrown for her own organization.

Colin came up behind her with an older, attractive woman on his arm. She was tastefully dressed in a knee-length black dress that showed off her trim waist, and her coppery brown hair fell in soft layers around her face. "Mom, you remember Savannah," Colin said.

The woman took Savannah's hand and said, "Oh yes, of course. We met at Colin's wine bar back in June. It's lovely to see you again, my dear. Just lovely."

"It's wonderful to see you again, too," Savannah said and blushed when Colin winked at her.

"We'd love to have you over to the house for dinner sometime soon," Colin's mother said.

"I'd like that," Savannah said.

Colin turned to Rayne. "And this is Savannah's roommate, Rayne."

Rayne held out her hand, and the woman gave it a squeeze. "Rayne Michael? You're the one who put this event together, right? You're Chase's friend. It's so nice to finally meet you."

Colin shifted uneasily, and Rayne was about to say she wasn't Chase's friend, but she caught herself. "It's nice to meet you, too, Mrs. Allison."

"Please, call me Bea. And I could just kick Chase for not being here. Especially after I had his tux dry-cleaned. I think I'll send him the bill when he gets back from Tibet or Nepal or wherever he flew off to."

Rayne was desperately trying to think of an excuse to walk away when Jeremy caught sight of them and hurried over. "Beatrice! I'm so glad you could make it."

"How could I stay away, especially after you sent those beautiful flowers."

"Most of these people are here because of you," he said. "We can't thank you enough."

"Oh, well, I'm always happy to support a good cause," she said, looking a little flustered. Rayne wasn't surprised to see that Jeremy's effect on women extended even to those who were older—and married. "I'm sorry my husband wasn't able to join me, but Saturday night is a busy one in the restaurant business."

"Of course," Jeremy said. "But Colin here has been doing a first-rate job. And Chase's photos are already drawing bids. So we owe an enormous debt to the Allison family."

"Where are Chase's photos?" she asked, and Jeremy led her away to show her.

"Seems there's no avoiding Chase tonight," Rayne said.

"Sorry, sweetie," Savannah said, and Colin snatched a glass of champagne from a passing waiter and handed it to Rayne.

"Nothing a little champagne can't fix," he said.

Rayne took a sip and nodded. Savannah watched another waiter go by carrying a tray of pastries stuffed with shrimp.

"What is that heavenly smell?" she said.

Colin laughed. "Come back to the kitchen with me and I'll fix you a sampler plate."

Savannah gave Rayne a questioning look, and Rayne waved a hand. "Go. Have fun. I'll be fine."

Rayne wandered around, mingling with the guests and answering questions about the art and the organization. The rooms were filling up, and people were laughing and talking and some were using the app Kyle had made to place bids while others used the laptops set up strategically for that purpose.

She found Kyle standing in front of Crystal's paintings punching buttons on his phone.

"That app of yours is just perfect," she said, and he jumped.

"Sorry, I didn't see you there," he said.

"Whatcha doing?" she asked in a teasing voice.

He glanced around furtively. "I figured if I bid on the pair a little above the reserve price, I'd still have some room to go up if anyone else bids."

"You really like them, huh?" she said. "And maybe the artist, too?" She nudged him in the ribs with her elbow.

Kyle's face turned pink with embarrassment. "My apartment walls are a little bare, and I just thought—"

"Whatever you say!" Rayne said.

When Crystal arrived a short time later, Rayne told her someone had already bid on her paintings, and she broke into a huge smile.

Rayne was on her third glass of champagne and thinking she really ought to eat something. The bids were humming along and everyone seemed to be enjoying themselves when she spotted Brandon gazing at Chase's photos. She took a deep breath and walked over.

He glanced up and then did a slow head-to-toe scan of her that made her uncomfortable—and a little pleased. By the expression on his face, he liked what he saw. He was wearing a tux with a red tie, and his thick blond hair was slicked back.

"You look stunning," he said.

She smiled. "Nice tux."

A waiter paused, and Brandon took two glasses of champagne from his tray and handed one to Rayne. She'd already had three—or was it four?—glasses, but it was really good champagne, and it was definitely taking the edge off her nervousness about the evening and helping her forget at least a little about Chase.

She took a sip of her drink as Brandon gestured toward Chase's photos. "These are great. Is the photographer here? I'd love to talk to him."

Rayne took another gulp of champagne. Why wouldn't everyone just shut up about Chase?

"I've been thinking about redoing the decor in our office," Brandon was saying, "and I think a series of photos like these might be just what I'm looking for."

Rayne downed the rest of her champagne. Then she leaned in with her fingertips braced against Brandon's chest and kissed him on the lips. Brandon looked stunned.

"He's not here, but Sheila has his contact info," Rayne said.

Then she started to walk away, swaying a little because of the champagne and her high heels, but Brandon caught her by the wrist and turned her back toward him. He glanced around to see if anyone was paying attention to them, but for once, Rayne didn't care. She was trying like hell to break the hold Chase seemed to have on her, and the kiss had, momentarily at least, exorcised him from her brain.

She knew she was flirting with danger, but she was feeling reckless, so she ran her fingers along the lapel of Brandon's tux jacket.

"Does this mean you'll go to dinner with me?" he asked.

"Where would we go?" she asked.

"Anywhere you want."

He was watching her intently, lips parted, and she had a sudden desire to drag him into the coat closet.

But then she thought of Chase, and the energy drained right out of her. She glanced toward the door, hoping against hope that he'd be standing there in his tux, hair falling in his eyes. Maybe he'd sent that text message from his apartment, maybe he'd changed his mind and never even left town. Or, better yet, maybe he'd gotten to Nepal and missed her so badly that he turned around and came right back.

But instead she saw Miss Ada sitting in a wheelchair with Rayne's roommate Carol behind her.

"I have to go," she said, handing Brandon her empty champagne glass.

She hurried over and bent down to give Ada a hug. "I'm so glad you came."

"Thank you for inviting me," Ada said. "This is a real treat. All these fancy people. I was getting sick of only seeing the inside of my own house."

"It's good to see you out and about," Rayne said. Then she straightened up and gave Carol a kiss on the cheek. "Thanks for bringing her. And you look smashing, by the way."

Carol was wearing a black velvet dress, and she'd swept her red hair up into a loose bun with wispy curls hanging down. "Thanks! It feels good to dress up for an event that I'm not responsible for. Speaking of which—nice job. Great turnout."

"Thanks. The real test will be whether we raise enough money." She took the handles of Miss Ada's wheelchair and steered her over to the makeshift bar. Brandon caught her eye as she passed, and she smiled but kept going.

She spent some time catching up with Carol and Miss Ada, then mingled with the other guests, carefully avoiding Brandon. The event was supposed to go till 11:00, but Kyle flagged her down at 10:30 and told her that if they closed the auctions down right now, they would have exceeded their goal.

"Are you sure?" she asked.

He showed her the results on his cell phone, where he was tracking the bids from a master dashboard.

"Oh my god!" She gave him a big hug and then ran to find Jeremy. He was standing with a cluster of people in the dining room.

"We did it!" she exclaimed.

He looked baffled for a split second then his handsome face broke into a big smile. He grabbed a fork and moved out to the main hallway, where he walked a little ways up the stairs and tapped his fork on his wine glass. Slowly the chatter died down, and people wandered over from the other rooms and gathered in the doorways.

"I've just been informed that we have met our fundraising target," he said.

A loud cheer went up, and Rayne thought her heart would burst from the excitement. They had done it. Her little seed of an idea—planted by Chase, but she wasn't thinking about that now—had grown into a strong, beautiful tree.

"We are so grateful for your support," Jeremy said when the noise had died down. "Our entire staff worked hard to make this happen, but I have to thank one person in particular."

He turned down at her, and her face flushed with embarrassment. "Rayne Michael came up with this plan when I was ready to throw in the towel, and she carried the idea through to the end. She has done a stellar job." He raised his glass. "To Rayne."

"Here, here!" people said and clinked their glasses and toasted her with champagne. Savannah came over and gave her a hug and then everyone was crowding around wanting to congratulate her and Jeremy, and her heart was full.

As people finally drifted away to check on their bids or head home, Brandon walked over and shook Jeremy's hand.

"Let me know what the final tally is," Brandon said. "And I'll write you a matching check."

"I appreciate that," Jeremy said. "Call Sheila next week, and she'll set up a lunch appointment."

"Will do," Brandon said. Then Jeremy turned his attention to another well-wisher, and Brandon faced Rayne.

"It was nice to see you tonight," he said.

He was as attractive as ever, but she was distracted by all the excitement and feeling fatigue creeping up on her. It was a good kind of exhaustion, but it wasn't the reckless thrill she'd felt earlier when she'd kissed him.

"You, too," she said.

"Walk me to the door?" he asked, and she nodded.

They stepped out onto the porch, and though the night was warm and cloudless, there was a slight chill to the air. He reached for her hand, his fingers barely brushing her palm, and kissed her lightly on the lips. She breathed in the familiar scent of his aftershave and sighed. It would be so easy to fall back into him.

"Call me about dinner," he whispered in her ear, and his hand trailed down her hip as he turned to go.

Chapter 17

The day after the gala, Rayne slept in till a decadent 10 a.m. She felt a twinge of sadness and regret that she wasn't waking up next to Chase at the Willard, but she brushed the thought away. She had been working her butt off, and she was going to enjoy herself today if it killed her.

The weather was perfect—bright blue sky and crisp fall air. Rayne had given the room at the Willard to Savannah and Colin, and Rayne was missing her this morning and feeling a little lonely and out of sorts now that the big event was over. Like the day after Christmas, she thought.

While Rayne was eating eggs and toast, Carol stumbled up the stairs from her bedroom in the basement.

"Is that coffee I smell?" she asked, her hair sticking up on one side.

"Help yourself," Rayne said. Carol filled a mug and sat down next to Rayne at the table, her hands wrapped around the mug as though she'd just emerged from a snowstorm.

"Thanks again for bringing Ada to the gala last night," Rayne said. "And for coming yourself."

"It was fun," Carol said, taking a sip of her coffee. "And I'm not just saying that. I had a nice time. And I won a really cool painting to boot."

She and Carol didn't hang out often because their schedules never seemed to overlap. Carol often worked odd hours in her job in donor relations at the Smithsonian. With Savannah spending so much time with Colin and now that Chase was out of the picture, Rayne was suddenly longing for company.

"What are you up to today?" Rayne asked.

"Nothing much," Carol said. "Laundry, cleaning, the usual Sunday fun."

"Let's take a walk down to the Mall. It's a beautiful day—"

Carol stared at her. "I work there every day. I don't want to spend my day off there."

"Yeah, but I bet you never even go to the National Gallery. And when's the last time you were in the Hirshhorn?"

Carol sighed. "You're right. I rarely even leave the office. Except for the Air and Space Museum. I've led so many visiting donors through there I know it better than the docents."

"Great! We can go as soon as you're ready. I'll spring for lunch."

Carol took a sip of her coffee and eyed Rayne's plate. "Make me some eggs first and you've got a deal."

Rayne smiled. "Absolutely!"

They spent the day wandering around the National Mall. They snapped pictures of each other on the carousel riding a palomino pony (Carol) and zebra (Rayne). Then they wandered around the National Gallery's sculpture garden, marveling at the enormous typewriter eraser, stainless steel tree, and flat house by Lichtenstein that managed to look three-dimensional.

In the basement of the Hirshhorn, they cocked their heads and puzzled over an installation of colored strings hanging from the ceiling.

"Seriously?" Carol said. "People get paid to do that?"

"I think it's a statement on man's inhumanity to man. See how the purple string is turning its back on the green string?" Rayne said with a straight face. Carol stared at her with an expression caught between disbelief and concern, and they both burst out laughing.

They stopped for lunch at the cafe downstairs by the National Gallery's East Wing, where they loaded their trays with smoked salmon melt sandwiches and slices of lemon meringue pie and sat down to eat within view of the cascade waterfall outside the window.

When Carol got up to refill their iced tea glasses, Rayne pulled out her phone to see if Savannah had texted her. She had a message, but it wasn't from Savannah. It was from Brandon.

Thinking of you. Have dinner with me Saturday?

When Carol came back with their drinks, Rayne was idly tapping her fingers on the table next to her phone. Carol sat down and gave her a quizzical look.

"What's up?" she asked.

"I got a text from Brandon, remember him?" Rayne had been living with Carol at the time, and Carol had witnessed some of the drama and Rayne's hysterics and depression afterward.

"Brandon the Cheater?" Carol said. "Let me guess—his marriage is on the rocks and he wants to see you again."

"Am I an idiot?"

"It depends. Are you thinking of going out with him?" Carol took a bite of her pie.

"Jeremy told me Brandon's wife has indeed moved out, so I have independent verification that he's not lying. About that part of it anyway."

"So this other thing, with Colin's brother—it's over for sure?" Carol took a drink of her tea, eyes on Rayne.

Rayne inhaled sharply and blinked away tears. "Yeah, it's over," she said softly.

Carol put her glass down. "Take it from a woman who's pushing thirty and still looking for Mr. Right: No guy is perfect. No guy comes without baggage. It's just a question of what you're willing to deal with. At a certain age and especially if you date older men, you're going to be dealing with ex-wives or ex-live-in girlfriends who might as well be ex-wives."

Carol scraped the rest of the meringue off her plate with her fork. "You and Brandon had an intense relationship. If you're still attracted to him, maybe there's something there. Your other guy is out of the picture, so why not go on a date and see what happens?"

Rayne smiled. "You're good at this. You should write an advice column."

"Ah yes, a popular career choice for snarky spinsters," Carol said with a laugh.

Rayne picked up her phone and typed: *OK. 7:00?*

Within moments, Brandon replied: *Yes. You name the place.*

She looked at Carol. "Do you ever take donors to fancy restaurants?"

"We're pretty budget-conscious," Carol said. "But there's this new place I've been thinking of trying. It's called the Carriage House Inn, and it's not far from our house, on Pennsylvania Avenue."

Rayne texted Brandon the name of the restaurant and immediately got a response: *I will be there. Can't wait to see you.*

"I don't suppose you have a fancy dress I could borrow?" Rayne said.

Carol thought about it. "You want sophisticated with a hint of sexy, but not slutty. I might have something. We can go through my closet when we get home."

"Thanks a bunch, Carol," Rayne said. "This is nice. I'm glad you came out with me today."

"Me, too." Carol smiled. "Does Brandon have any recently divorced friends?"

Rayne laughed. "Let's see how this first date goes before we start double dating."

Savannah was not pleased when Rayne told her she'd made a date with Brandon. But Rayne finally convinced her that it was just dinner—albeit at a restaurant Rayne could never afford on her own—and that she would take it slow.

"I'm just worried that you haven't given yourself a chance to get over this thing with Chase," Savannah said. "You could be rebounding big time."

Rayne had thought of that and rejected it, mostly because she already knew Brandon. Wasn't rebounding something you did with a stranger?

"I'll be fine," she said.

Chase had no idea how long he'd slept—could have been minutes, could have been days—because he only seemed to wake up when it was dark outside. His bed was a tangle of sheets, and he was aware of having knocked his phone to the floor at one point while he was trying to text Colin and rolling over on top of a water bottle. His headache was blinding, and he was still feeling so nauseated that he finally crawled out of bed and laid down on the floor, which didn't move as much as the bed.

He heard someone knocking and calling his name, but it sounded like they were at the other end of a very long tunnel.

"Rayne?" he said, his voice a hoarse croak. He had just been talking to her. Or maybe dreaming about her. But she seemed real.

He opened his eyes a slit, his parched lips breaking into a painful smile. But it wasn't Rayne. It was a Nepali girl—Maya, from the guest house in Kathmandu. What was she doing here?

She knelt down beside him. "How long have you been like this?" She put her hand on his forehead, and it felt cool and soft, the most delicious sensation next to a glass of water.

He didn't answer, so she asked, "When did you get back from Chitwan? I didn't see you come in."

Chitwan. Elephants and rhinos and antelope. Hot, beautiful Chitwan. And the big Texan on the bus. How long ago had that been?

"I don't know," he finally said.

"Have you been sick to your stomach?"

He nodded, but only a little. The pain in his head made his eyes water.

"Headache?"

"Everything hurts," he said.

"Chills?"

"Malaria relapse, nurse. Forgot to bring my pills."

She touched his arm. "We need to get you back into bed. You'll only feel worse if you lie on the floor."

He looked at her through half-open eyes, lit up like an angel with the sun behind her. "This is a nice dream," he said. "I'm glad you're in it."

She shook her head, smiling. "It's not a dream, Chase Allison. You're in my guest house in Kathmandu and you have malaria and I'm going to call a doctor."

She grabbed both his hands, pulled him to his feet, and gently guided him back to the bed. He sat upright long enough for her to untangle the sheets and then he collapsed onto his side and curled up.

"That man Roy has been calling for you," she said as she pulled the blankets up to his shoulders. "No one knew you were here, and you didn't answer your door or phone."

Chase was confused. He'd already gone on that gig. Or did he just dream it? Or was he dreaming that he'd missed it to remind himself to wake up and call Roy?

"What day is it?" he asked.

She bent down and picked up his phone and the water bottle and set them on the stand next to his bed. "Thursday," she said.

"No, that can't be right," Chase said. "I just got back. And it's daylight so it must only be"—he thought hard—"Monday."

"I assure you it's Thursday," she said. Then she looked at him. "You mean you haven't eaten in three days?"

"I guess not," he said.

"I'll call the doctor and if he won't come here, I'll go to him and get the medicine. And I'll send Mama up with some broth in the meantime."

"I don't want you to go to all that trouble. I'll go to the doctor's." He tried to sit up, but she gently pushed him back down.

"I'll do it," she said. "I don't mind."

He smiled. "You haven't turned twenty-one while I was out, have you?"

"You haven't been sleeping that long. I'll be back soon."

He drifted off to sleep without even hearing the door close behind her. Sometime later, her mother came in with a bowl of broth. Chase sat up in bed with his back propped against the wall and ate the broth one slow spoonful at a time. It felt good to eat, but it was exhausting, and as soon as she took the bowl back, he laid down and closed his eyes.

At some point, Maya woke him. She had a bottle of pills and a glass of water. He dutifully sat up to take the pills, and she brushed his sweaty hair away from his forehead as he drank the water. Then it was a cycle of sleep and medicine and broth, which gradually had bits of tofu, vegetables, and noodles. Sometimes it was Maya and sometimes it was her mother who brought the broth, and once Maya's younger brother came to give him his medicine.

On Saturday evening, Savannah stuck around while Rayne got dressed in a slinky black cocktail dress that Carol had found at the back of her closet.

"I only wore it one time," she said. "It just wasn't me."

It fit Rayne perfectly. She pinned up her hair, leaving some long strands hanging down around her face and neck, and put on a matching set of coin pearl necklace and earrings.

"You look gorgeous," Savannah said.

Rayne grabbed her beaded handbag and swiped on some coppery red lipstick.

"Think this is too much for a casual get-to-know-each-other-again dinner?" Rayne asked.

"Yes," Carol and Savannah said at the same time.

Rayne grinned. "Good. I was going for a little bit of an 'eat your heart out' vibe."

"You go, girl!" Carol said.

"I feel like such a grown-up," Rayne said.

"Just please be careful," Savannah said. "And text me immediately if anything goes wrong."

"Or right," Carol said with a wink, and Savannah frowned.

"Text me when you get home," Savannah said.

Rayne's phone beeped, and she glanced at it, thinking it was Brandon. But the message was from Chase. She stared at it for a moment then held her phone out for Savannah and Carol to see.

missU siick.

"What's that about?" Savannah asked.

"It's like those spam emails you get when someone's hijacked a friend's account," Carol said.

"He sent me one the night of the gala," Rayne said. "His messages are usually much more legible."

"Is he saying he's sick or he's missing you siiiiicccckkk?" Savannah said. "You know, like slang for good?"

"Missing me good?" Rayne said.

"Maybe Carol's right and someone else is texting you from his account. Like a teenager."

Rayne set the phone to vibrate. "He can text all he wants. I have a dinner date."

Chapter 18

Half an hour later, Rayne stepped inside the restaurant and took a moment to get her bearings. The walls were of exposed old bricks, thick beams ran along the ceiling, and the wooden flooring was worn in a way that spoke of decades of activity. A couple of sofas sat along the walls, and stuffed armchairs were grouped around small tables. She walked over to the hostess stand and was surprised, and flustered, to see Chase's sister Jessica.

"I didn't know you worked here," Rayne said.

Jessica smiled, looking professional in her black skirt and white blouse. "My dad just opened this place a few weeks ago, so I'm helping out until he can get a permanent manager. Mom says he's been trying to con Chase into taking over, but that's a losing battle if I ever saw one."

Rayne smiled but didn't trust her voice to speak. Clearly, Jessica didn't know about her and Chase. For once, she was grateful for secrecy.

"You did an awesome job with the gala the other night," Jessica said, then looked at Rayne like she was just noticing how she was dressed. "Oh, crap, here I am rattling on and you must be here for a date—right?"

"Yes, as a matter of fact, I'm meeting a man, Brandon Wallace? I'm pretty sure he made a reservation."

Jessica stared at her for a moment. "I'm being way unprofessional here, but wow. I seated him about fifteen minutes ago. He's pretty hot for an older guy."

Rayne was blushing and suddenly hoping that Jessica would tell Chase about her date, whenever he got back from Nepal.

And then she reminded herself that tonight wasn't about Chase.

Jessica put her smooth, professional smile back in place. "Let me show you to your table," she said.

She led Rayne into the dining room, which was small but cozy with iron chandeliers and more brick. Brandon was at a table next to a fireplace that was soot-stained from years, maybe centuries of use. He stood when he saw her and gave her a kiss on the cheek.

Jessica said, "Your waitress will be right with you."

Rayne sat down across from Brandon, and he immediately reached over and squeezed her hand. "I'm so glad you came. You look beautiful."

"Thanks," she said. "You look pretty good yourself."

He was wearing dress pants and an expensive-looking shirt, unbuttoned at the throat. His hair was neatly trimmed, and he was freshly shaven. She thought he looked a little nervous. She liked that. It meant he cared how the evening went, and he wasn't taking anything for granted.

The waitress stopped by and they ordered crab-stuffed sole and a bottle of chardonnay. When she left, Brandon said, "I got the final fundraising numbers from Jeremy. I just need to transfer some money, and we should be all set."

Rayne smiled, grateful to have work to talk about. She was feeling nervous, too. She asked about his business, and they were soon chatting like old friends.

An hour later, she was feeling tipsy and very relaxed. The date had gone better than she'd hoped. Brandon was still a little intense, but he had slowly relaxed, too. He had been funny and thoughtful and interested in what she had to say. This could work, she thought.

They ordered crème brûlée and coffee, and as they waited for their dessert, Brandon said, "I figured I might be out late tonight so I reserved a room at the Hyatt, just in case I don't feel like driving all the way back to Annapolis." He took a sip of his wine. "They still do a fantastic breakfast buffet."

Rayne's heart jumped a little. They'd gone there a few times when they'd had their fling. She remembered the brunch well, mostly because they'd usually eaten it in bed, naked. She could almost taste the ripe strawberries and his fingers as he placed one in her mouth—

"Really?" she said.

He slid his foot toward her under the table and pressed his calf against hers. Then he reached across the table, turned over her hand, and traced a finger lightly across her palm and up her wrist, a sensation that always set her off—and he knew it.

"Stay with me tonight," he said.

She bit her lip to stop a little moan of pleasure from escaping. He leaned forward and lifted her hand to kiss her palm and then froze, his eyes on something behind her.

"Shit," he said under his breath and let go of her hand.

Rayne twisted around in her chair thinking maybe Jeremy was there. Who else would he care about seeing them together? Instead, she saw a woman talking to Jessica—a stunning woman wearing a black blazer over a low-cut lacy white top, skin-tight jeans, and high heels.

"I never imagined that she'd come here. She's supposed to be in Annapolis."

Suddenly Rayne didn't need to ask who "she" was.

"Your wife is here?" she said.

Brandon nodded, still watching Yvonne and not looking at Rayne, who felt a coldness seeping into her bones. And a searing anger.

"What difference does it make?" she asked. "You've split up."

But the look on Brandon's face told her that things were far from over between him and Yvonne.

"Let's go," he said, tossing his napkin on the table.

"We haven't had our dessert," Rayne protested, though that wasn't the real reason she wanted to stay put.

But he wasn't listening to her. "I'll pay the bill on the way out. With any luck, she won't even see us."

"Brandon, this is silly."

He started to stand up but then sank back in his chair. "It's too late."

Rayne looked up just as Yvonne broke away from Jessica to walk over to their table.

"Brandon," she said. "I didn't think this was your kind of place."

"Yvonne," he said, gazing up at her.

"Aren't you going to introduce me to your date?" Yvonne said.

"Oh, Rayne is just a colleague. She put on a very successful fundraiser at CACC, and we were having a congratulatory dinner."

Rayne stared at him in open-mouthed surprise. Beyond being an out-and-out lie, his answer had been too smooth, almost rehearsed.

"I'm glad to hear that," Yvonne said. "She looks a little young even for you, Brandon."

Rayne's face flushed red hot and she was about to ask what Yvonne meant by that when the waitress walked over with their dessert and coffee.

Yvonne said, "I'll leave you two to enjoy the rest of your meal. It was a pleasure meeting you, Rayne."

Then she sashayed off to rejoin Jessica, who was looking at Rayne with a sympathetic expression that said she had a pretty good idea of what was going on. Brandon watched Yvonne go, and Rayne felt pure, hot rage boiling up. For once, she didn't tell herself not to over-react. For once, she intended to say exactly what was in her head.

"Why did you lie and tell her this wasn't a date?" Rayne demanded.

Brandon's head swiveled toward her. "Trust me, it's better this way."

She put her napkin on the table. "I think I'll just go set her straight, tell her that we're headed to the Hyatt for the night."

He grabbed her hand to stop her then immediately let go and glanced across the room to Yvonne's table.

"You are pathetic," Rayne said.

He leaned toward her, keeping his voice low. "I didn't want her to know I was seeing someone. Not until we settle on how to divide our finances and the house, and I've got my business to think of."

"I don't think you're in a hurry to do any of that," Rayne said. "I can't believe what an idiot I've been."

"Please keep your voice down," Brandon said. Their coffee and dessert sat untouched on the table, but he got to his feet. "Let's just go. We can talk about this at the hotel."

She laughed, a sharp, bitter sound that made him glance yet again in Yvonne's direction. His wife wasn't paying attention, but a few of the other diners looked over at them.

"Please don't make a scene," Brandon said.

Rayne was feeling distinctly in the mood to make a scene for the first time in her life, but she saw Jessica watching them from the hostess stand and decided she didn't need this to get back to Chase. Besides, she could just as easily have it out with Brandon on the sidewalk.

She slowly got to her feet and followed him out of the dining area. While he paid the bill at the bar, Jessica mouthed You OK? Rayne nodded and flashed her best fake smile. Then Brandon took her by the elbow and steered her outside.

She shook free of him as soon as they were on the sidewalk. A cluster of people stood right in front of the restaurant so she walked on a little ways. Brandon kept pace with her, and when she moved toward the curb to hail a cab, he caught her by the wrist and spun her toward him. She lost her balance and fell against his chest.

He instantly put his arms around her. "That's better," he said, smiling and pressing her against him. "I'm sorry I had to lie back there. Things with Yvonne are complicated, and they probably will be for a long time. But that doesn't mean you and I can't have some fun together."

Rayne twisted free of his grip and stepped back a pace. A look of surprise crossed his face, quickly followed by irritation.

"What did she mean when she said I was too young even for you?" she asked. "You said I was the only one."

He sighed. "She was just trying to upset you." He moved toward her, and she backed away again.

"Why did Yvonne leave you?" she demanded.

"Rayne—"

"Just tell me!"

"Lower your voice," Brandon said, looking over his shoulder at the people standing in front of the restaurant. "OK, fine. There was a girl at the office. It was over before it even started. But Yvonne found out."

"So you lied about that, too. Have you ever said one true thing to me?"

"I was telling the truth when I said you look beautiful tonight. And I want to take you back to the Hyatt." He closed the distance between them and trailed his fingers up her arm until they came to rest on her collarbone. He toyed with her necklace. "I've been dying to get my hands on you since I saw you at the gala last week."

The way he had pivoted from her to Yvonne and back again made her realize that he didn't want to be with her necessarily, he just didn't want to be alone, and Rayne happened to be handy. And easily seduced.

"What about Yvonne?" she said.

He tucked a strand of hair behind her ear. "I don't think she'd be into a threesome, but I appreciate the thought," he joked.

She pushed him away. "You can keep your disgusting fantasies to yourself. I'm going home."

He reached for her arm, but she sidestepped out of his reach.

"If Yvonne walked out that door right now and said she wanted you to take her home, what would you do?" Rayne asked.

"That's not fair," he said. "For one thing, she isn't about to do that—"

"You can't have both of us," Rayne said. "It doesn't work that way, at least not for long. It didn't go so well the last time you tried."

"You're the one who broke it off."

"Because you're married!"

"Jesus, Rayne, what's gotten into you?"

"I'm suddenly seeing things crystal clear. You aren't interested in having a relationship with me. You just want someone to kill time with until you can figure out how to get Yvonne back."

"It's not like that," he said. "I do like you. I want to be with you."

"Just not out in the open," she said. "Why the Hyatt? Why not your house in Annapolis?"

"I can't take you there. Not yet."

"Then when?"

"I don't know! What difference does it make? The Hyatt is much nicer anyway."

"That's what cheaters do. They go to a hotel instead of their home."

A taxi came around the corner, and she stepped out into the street to hail it, prepared to stand in front of it if she had to. The driver swung over to the curb, and as she pulled the door open, she looked back at Brandon.

"You don't deserve either of us."

Then she got in the cab and slammed the door, and when the car drove off, she didn't even look back.

When Rayne got home, she was shaking with rage. She kicked off her shoes and carried them up the stairs, texting Savannah as she went. *Date was a disaster. Home now.*

Savannah texted back immediately: *I'm on my way.*

No, stay where you are. I'm fine.

Rayne reached her bedroom and tossed her shoes in the closet and took off her dress. She'd have to get it dry cleaned. She didn't want a trace of Brandon's aftershave in her closet.

Savannah texted back: *Brunch @ Zipped tomorrow?? 10:00?*

You're on! Rayne texted as she walked to the bathroom.

I could be there in 30...

Love you! But I'm good. Going to take a hot bath and go to bed. See you tomorrow.

The next morning, Savannah was already seated at a window table at Zipped when Rayne got there. After a quick hug, Savannah said, "Colin is bringing us mimosas."

Just then, Colin walked over with the drinks. "Hey, Rayne," he said. "You doing OK?"

"Yeah, I'm fine," she said with a smile. She took a sip of the drink, and the fizziness perked her up. "Good call on the mimosas."

When she'd woken up that morning, her feeling of elation at having told Brandon off had evaporated, and she felt tired and sad and lonely. She'd been thinking about Chase more than she wanted to, and she had a sudden urge to get out of town.

She and Savannah walked over to the buffet and loaded their plates with Belgian waffles and scrambled eggs and fresh donuts. Rayne added a couple slices of cantaloupe to keep her conscience clean. When they got back to the table and started eating, Savannah said, "So do you want to talk about it?"

Rayne sopped up maple syrup with a chunk of waffle. "Not much to tell," she said. "We had a nice dinner, he asked me to go back to his hotel, and then his wife showed up."

Savannah dropped her fork with a clatter. "Are you kidding me?"

Rayne shook her head as she ate the syrup-saturated chunk of waffle. "He lied and told her we weren't on a date. Turns out she left him because she found out he was messing around with a younger woman at the office."

"What did you do?" Savannah asked.

"I told him I knew he didn't want me, he just didn't want to be alone, and then I got a cab out of there."

"Oh, Rayney, I'm so sorry."

"It's OK, really." She broke off a piece of donut. "He's totally out of my system now. I just wish Jessica hadn't been there."

Savannah gave her a puzzled look. "Colin's sister?"

"She works at the restaurant. Apparently it's a new Allison Inc. joint. I would have been fine with her telling Chase I had a date with a hot older guy, but she saw the interaction with Yvonne and she knows things were frosty between Brandon and me when we left."

"I'm sure she'd lie to Chase if you asked her to," Savannah said with a smile.

"She didn't even know Chase and me were a thing, and I'd rather not tell her."

Savannah nodded. "So you're still thinking about him?" she asked quietly.

Rayne crumpled up the piece of donut in her fingers and dropped the crumbs onto the plate. "Maybe. Yes. More than I probably should."

"He really got inside your head, huh?" Savannah said as she picked at the sprinkles on her own donut.

"Head. Heart. Whatever." Rayne took a long drink of her mimosa.

"Heart?"

"Yeah, even though he's a player who can't stick with one woman for more than a week. Even though I knew all that going in." Rayne played with the stem of her glass. "Before he took off, it felt...different. It felt real. He said he wanted a relationship, and I believed him. And I started to fall for him."

She turned to gaze out the window, feeling too emotional to look at Savannah and see the sympathy in her face. She could sense Savannah studying her and braced herself for a well-deserved "I told you so" lecture.

After a few minutes, Savannah said, "For what it's worth, I could tell something was different about you while you were with him. You seemed...lighter somehow. And Colin said Chase seemed different, too. He was convinced it was because of a woman, and he told me she must be pretty special because Chase was really excited about her. Bubbly even." Savannah reached out and squeezed Rayne's hand. "Obviously, he was right about the woman being special."

Rayne looked at her with a sad smile. "Yep, I'm pretty special. So special that he turned tail and ran literally to the other side of the planet without a second thought." She gave Savannah's hand a squeeze in return. "Now I just have to get over it."

"Give yourself some time," Savannah said.

Rayne went back to gazing out the window. The trees were changing colors, though there was still lots of green. "My mom emailed me some photos from Vermont," she said. "It's absolutely gorgeous up there this time of year."

"Maybe you should go for a visit," Savannah said.

"I was thinking about it. I could really use a change of scenery, and I'm sure Jeremy would let me take some time off. Of course, it means dealing with my hippie parents, but that's a small price to pay."

"Your parents are awesome," Savannah said, smiling and biting into a chocolate croissant.

"Easy for you to say. They didn't drag you all over creation while you were growing up. You got to live in the same neighborhood and go through school with all the same friends."

"Sure, but you got to see the world and have all those adventures. Lots of people would love to have that."

"Yeah, maybe you're right," Rayne said, suddenly missing her parents. Then she smiled and felt some of the tension easing. "I'll bring you back some real maple syrup."

"Oh, and those little maple sugar candies pressed into the shape of leaves!"

"You got it!"

Colin walked over to their table, phone in hand, and Rayne said, "I'm taking orders for souvenirs from Vermont. Want a T-shirt or a baseball cap?"

Colin looked at her blankly. "You're going to Vermont?"

"To visit her parents," Savannah said. "Is something wrong?"

Colin shook his head. "I got a garbled text message from Chase a couple days ago."

Rayne took a sip of her mimosa. "I've gotten a couple strange texts from him, too."

"He just sent a message saying he's got malaria."

"That's pretty serious, isn't it?" Savannah said.

Colin nodded. "People die from it. He had it once before a couple years ago. This could be a relapse brought on by stress or fatigue."

"But he's not that sick, right?" Rayne said, feeling a flash of concern.

"I think he's getting better." Colin gazed out the window. "It figures he'd get deathly ill when he's in Kathmandu."

"It's not like people get malaria in France," Savannah said as she buttered a roll. "Heck, if he was in Paris, I'd go get him myself! With you, of course, sweetie," she added, smiling up at Colin.

"Chase is a pretty resourceful guy," Rayne said. "And they do have doctors in Kathmandu. I'm sure he'll be fine." Still, she couldn't resist a brief fantasy of flying to Nepal and showing up at his hotel room, like a romantic Florence Nightingale come to save the day. But then she reminded herself that he wasn't hers to rescue.

She stood up. "I'm going to head home. I want to email Jeremy and check the Amtrak schedule and do some laundry."

"I'll go with you," Savannah said.

"What do we owe you?" Rayne said to Colin, knowing his answer.

"You're hilarious, Rayne," he said as he always did when she offered to pay.

She tucked a ten under her glass by way of a tip. "I will never get used to that."

Savannah wrapped her arms around Colin and stretched up to give him a noisy kiss. "This body and free food? How did I get so lucky?"

He smiled and kissed the top of her head before letting her go. "Have a good trip, Rayne. And I wouldn't say no to a baseball cap."

"You got it!" she said, and something in his smile reminded her of Chase. But she refused to hold that against him.

Chapter 19

A couple days later, Chase was finally well enough to walk down the hall for a much-needed shower. Afterward, as he sat on the bed in clean clothes, hair freshly washed, and face clean shaven, Maya set a tray with a bowl of curry, a plate of naan, and a cup of tea on his bedside table.

The meal smelled and tasted better than anything he'd ever eaten.

"Have you run out of family members to look after me?" he joked as he tore off a chunk of naan. "I haven't met your grandparents yet."

"They never leave their village," she said with a smile. "Otherwise, they would have helped, too."

She was turning to go, and he reached out and touched her arm. "I can't thank you enough. You all really went out of your way to help me."

She shrugged. "It's what people do for each other. They would do the same in America, right?"

"I don't know. I always seem to be somewhere other than home. But never long enough to get to know anyone."

"You know me and my family," she said.

"Yeah, I guess I do."

"Who took care of you the last time you had malaria?"

"My brother Colin. I made it back to the States before I got sick that time."

He vaguely remembered trying to text Colin that he was sick. But it wasn't as though Colin would have been worried. Chase had told him he'd be gone for weeks, and he rarely checked in anyway. He picked up his phone, but the battery was dead. He looked around on the floor, found the charger, and plugged the phone in.

"I should send him a message to let him know I'm OK," Chase said.

It sounded a little strange to his ears, but Maya nodded as though it was the most natural thing in the world. She picked up the tray of dishes and headed for the door.

"Hey, did Roy Fellows call by any chance?" Chase asked.

She shook her head and left. He had a sinking feeling that he'd blown the assignment.

A little while later, when his phone was partially charged, he got confirmation that he had indeed blown it. There were multiple, increasingly irritable texts from Roy, who finally left a voice message saying that since he couldn't get hold of Chase, he was going to find another photographer. Chase looked at the date on his watch. Roy had left Kathmandu days ago.

"Shit!"

He couldn't believe he'd come all this way and then lost out on the assignment. He'd gotten malaria for nothing, he'd broken things off with Rayne for nothing. Even though he was physically feeling better, the thought of traveling around Asia on his own was exhausting. He was restless and unhappy and something else, but it took him a moment to identify it.

Then it came to him. He wanted to go home.

"That's a new one," he said out loud.

In all his years of traveling, he had never had the urge to go home before the assignment was over or he'd satisfied his curiosity about a side trip. But now he wanted to walk into Zipped so Colin could serve him a cold beer and Diana could bring him a plate of wings. And Rayne could sit down beside him. He longed to look into her smoldering gray eyes and watch her shyly tuck her hair behind her ear the way she did when he looked at her a certain way or laughed at one of her jokes.

They had only made love that one spectacular night because he'd agreed to keep their relationship a secret and they'd never had a chance to be alone again. What an idiot. This might be easier to bear if they'd slept together at least once more. Maybe twice. Or however long it took for him to get that itch to move on. Though part of him wondered if he might never have gotten that itch with her.

Maybe it was the wine but that one night with him, Rayne had been so free, so uninhibited, so open. Chase suspected that was the real Rayne, the one she kept hidden away. He'd caught another glimpse of that fire the day he told her he was going to Nepal, and he still felt singed by it. He suspected that not many people saw that side of her, and maybe that meant something.

But now he'd never know.

His phone was still charging, so he decided to go to an Internet cafe down the street and catch up on some email. He glanced through his text messages and saw that he had texted Rayne twice, but the messages were garbled, and even he had to think about what he'd meant to say. She hadn't responded to either one, and he couldn't really blame her. But he did have a series of texts from Colin asking what was up in response to some truly incomprehensible messages from Chase.

He sent a quick note back saying he was recovering from malaria and would email him momentarily. Then he grabbed his laptop bag and headed for the door. But he didn't even open it before dizziness overwhelmed him and he had to sit down. He closed his eyes and waited for the queasiness and frustration to pass. They didn't. So after a few minutes he laid down on the bed fully clothed. The Internet cafe and emailing Colin and finding a flight back home would have to wait.

He slept straight through the night and the next morning felt strong enough to try again. He made it down the stairs and stopped at the front desk to catch his breath and say hello to Maya.

"I'm going to the Internet cafe up the street," he said. "If I'm not back by noon, come and get me." He was only half joking.

"You sure you're up for this?" she asked.

He'd gotten a good look at himself in the bathroom mirror that morning. He was pale, and he'd lost enough weight that his clothes were a little baggy.

"Nope," he said. "That's why I'm telling you where I'm going, so you'll know to look for me between here and there."

She smiled. "The new and improved Chase Allison."

"I might need mouth-to-mouth resuscitation, so don't send your brother." He paused. "Or your parents."

"I'm still seventeen," she said, and he was disappointed that she'd stopped the game instead of him. "Besides, I'm not sure Rayne would approve."

"Rayne?" His heart skipped a beat, but it wasn't the malaria.

"You called for her. You called me by that name more than once when you were feverish," Maya said. "I didn't know you had a girl back in America."

"I don't," he said. "Not anymore anyway."

"Then why was her name the only coherent word you said, and why are you now so anxious to get to the Internet?"

Chase could actually feel himself blushing. That had to be another first. "Has anyone ever told you that you're too clever for your own good?"

"I am a dangerous woman," she said sweetly.

At the cafe, Chase fired up his laptop and sent Colin an email explaining in more detail what had happened—that he'd gotten malaria and missed the assignment and that he was going to book a flight home as soon as possible. And he asked how the gala had gone.

While he was going through his flight options, Colin emailed back. Chase had to smile at his response: "You should have told me, bro. I would have hopped on a plane and brought you home." Like Colin would ever leave his restaurants long enough to take a flight anywhere.

He said the gala was a smashing success and all of Chase's photos sold for a lot of money, more than the price he'd set. Chase thought about asking Colin to Skype with him—he had an urge to see his brother—but he knew he looked like hell and he didn't want to alarm him. So he sent an email back asking how Rayne was doing and whether she'd been hanging around Brian Walrus at the gala.

By the time Colin responded, Chase had booked a flight for

the day after tomorrow, which meant he'd be home Wednesday night.

"The guy's name is Brandon," Colin wrote. "I didn't see them interact during the gala, but they had dinner at Dad's new restaurant. Jess saw them. When are you coming home?"

Chase sat back in his chair. He didn't put much stock in dreams, but he couldn't shake the hallucinations he'd had when he was sick. *Chase ran away, but I'm glad you're here.*

Chase sent Colin his flight information. "I'll be home on Wednesday. If you see Rayne, would you tell her I was asking about her?"

He waited another half hour, caught up on his other email, and read the front-page stories on the BBC site, but Colin didn't email back. Reluctantly, he packed up his laptop and headed back to the guest house.

Two days later, he was at the front desk with his bags packed. It was tougher than he'd expected to say goodbye to Maya and her family, and he got a lump in his throat when they all came out from behind the counter to give him a hug.

Maya hugged him last. She felt light and supple and so very young in his arms, and she had to stand on tiptoe to put her hands on his shoulders.

"I think you saved my life," he said in a low voice, close to her ear.

"You're welcome," she said with a smile.

He took a taxi to the airport, and after he checked in for his flight, he paced around for a long time with his phone in his hand until he finally broke down and texted Rayne: *Flying home today. I've been thinking about you. Can I stop by and see you tomorrow?*

He kept the phone in his hand, willing it to beep with a response, but then it was time to board the plane and he turned it off and put it away.

Chapter 20

On Wednesday morning, Rayne showered, dressed, ate a quick bowl of cereal, and headed out the front door. She had a backpack full of magazines and snacks on her shoulder for the long train ride, and she was wheeling her suitcase behind her.

The sun was just starting to come up when she walked along 2nd Street toward Union Station. There were few people on the sidewalks at this hour, but the streets were filling up with traffic. It was a cool morning, and she was glad she'd put on her oversized wool sweater. Plus, she knew it would be even colder when she got to Vermont that evening.

Jeremy had readily approved her request to take a few days off and told her she was welcome to log in remotely and work from Vermont as long as she wanted, which made her think she might stay a couple of weeks.

When she got to the station, she bought a chai latte, found the gate for her train, and sat down to wait. Commuters were bustling by from the subway, and shopkeepers were opening up their kiosks for the day. She was glad not to be part of that activity. She was looking forward to catching up with her parents, and she was looking forward to a long train ride when she didn't have to do anything. She could read, sleep, or stare out the window. It sounded so therapeutic that she might just be cured of Chase by the time she got to Brattleboro.

When the train was ready, she walked down the platform past where everyone else was getting on and found a window seat in a less populated car near the front. She was all settled in with a copy of Time magazine on her lap and drinking the last of her chai as the train pulled out of the station. She watched the city glide by, the sun shining brightly now, and felt oddly centered. She was calm but excited, and for a split second, she thought she understood Chase's wanderlust.

Baltimore, Philly, New York City passed by. She dozed and munched on pita bread and hummus and read three magazines. She and Savannah texted back and forth, and then Rayne noticed a message that had come in earlier from someone else. She tapped on her screen and felt a flutter in her stomach when she saw that it was from Chase.

Flying home today. I've been thinking about you. Can I stop by and see you tomorrow?

She gazed out the window. They were somewhere in Connecticut, passing a marsh ringed by trees whose leaves had turned bronze and orange. He didn't need to know she was on a train to Vermont. And she didn't need to know that he'd been thinking about her. Maybe they could be friends at some point, and for Savannah and Colin's sake, she'd have to learn to be civil around him. But she didn't have to play his games. What did he possibly hope to gain by telling her he'd been thinking about her?

Finally she typed back: *Sorry, I'm busy.*

Rayne arrived in Brattleboro just after 5 p.m. When she got off the train, her parents were waiting right beside the tracks. No security checkpoint, no armed guards, not even any platform to speak of. The station was the ground floor of an art museum, facing the Connecticut River and New Hampshire.

She hugged her parents tight, then her dad took her suitcase and led the way to their beat-up pickup truck in the parking lot.

"I can't believe you still have this thing!" Rayne said.

"Your father has replaced so many of the parts over the years that everything's new except the outer shell," her mother said.

Her wavy brown hair was pulled back in a loose ponytail and held in place with a red bandana. Her hair looked darker than usual, and there wasn't any gray.

"Did you color your hair?" Rayne asked, incredulous.

Her mom was one of the least vain women she knew, but it helped that she had a natural, simple style and skin that seemed to resist wrinkling. But Rayne had never known her to go to the trouble of dyeing her hair.

Even in the fading daylight, Rayne could tell her mom was blushing. "I was going gray, and my friend up the road offered to color it for me." Then she leaned closer to Rayne and whispered. "Your father likes it. Says I look ten years younger."

Rayne laughed and glanced over at her father as he slid her suitcase into the back of the truck. He looked the same as always—same short beard and mustache, salt and pepper now, and close-cropped hair. But today he was wearing a knit hat in fluorescent orange.

"Nice hat, Dad," Rayne said as she squeezed into the front seat between her parents.

"Turkey-hunting season's about to start," he said. "Wearing hunter orange is the easiest way to keep from getting shot."

He started the engine and moved the creaky gear shift on the steering wheel. A certifiable antique, she thought, and wondered what the Smithsonian's American history museum would pay for it. She made a mental note to ask Carol.

"The easiest way to keep from getting shot would be to stay indoors," she said with a shiver. "It's way colder up here than D.C."

"You'll get used to it," her dad said as they pulled out of the parking lot. "Especially after a couple of mornings of getting up early to feed the chickens."

Rayne gave her mom a pleading look. "You knew your father would put you to work," she said. "And chickens are easy. Next time you come up, we're hoping to have some sheep."

They drove up Main Street through the heart of Brattleboro's historic district, past a food co-op the size of a grocery store, an outdoor outfitter, a couple fine art galleries, second-hand stores, and funky one-of-a-kind shops. They had barely gotten on Highway 91 before her dad turned off, and the truck bounced along a road that looked like it hadn't been repaved since the fifties. But it beat the dirt road her dad turned onto next.

"Sheep sound kind of permanent," Rayne said. "You guys must really like it here."

"Yes, I guess we do," her mother said.

Rayne was starting to see why. When they turned into the driveway, the sun had nearly set. Chickens scattered in front of the truck, and her dad slowed to a crawl to let them get out of the way. The house was small but newer than Rayne had expected, and it looked cozy with the smoke curling up from the chimney. It sat on a little rise, and down the hill was a barn and a chicken coop. The property was ringed by a forest of evergreens and ghostly birches and bright red maples.

As they got out of the truck, she spotted a small cluster of trees near the house. "Are those apple trees?" she asked.

"Yes," her mother said. "And a couple of pears. We've still got some of the fruit in the house if you want to try it."

"You guys could have your own farmer's market," Rayne said. "How come we never lived anyplace like this when I was growing up?"

She followed her mother as she expertly shooed the chickens toward the coop. Her mom scooped some cracked corn from a metal can and handed it to Rayne. "Here, you feed them."

Rayne stepped into the coop and the hens followed her, bobbing their heads as they maneuvered up the wooden ramp. The inside of the coop was surprisingly clean of chicken crap, but feathers were mixed in with the straw on the ground, and it had the warm smell of animals. She put the food in a tray on the floor and the hens bustled around her, clucking and pecking at each other as they jockeyed for position. She carefully moved back to avoid stepping on any of them.

Then she went outside, and her mother latched the door closed. "We've lost a few to foxes, so we're thinking it's time to get a dog," she said.

"First chickens, now sheep and a dog! When did you guys turn into homesteaders?"

Her mother laughed and led her up the hill to the house. It was just as cozy and warm inside as it had looked from the outside. And it smelled of cinnamon candles and bread baking. The large central room doubled as living room and kitchen, and she saw that her dad had stashed her suitcase in the tiny bedroom nearest the kitchen. Now he was adding wood to the antique iron stove at the center of the house.

"You think you would have liked living on a farm when you were a kid?" her mom asked as she took off her boots by the door. Rayne followed suit and took off her own shoes. "I thought maybe you were a city girl at heart."

"I would have preferred a farm like this to that commune in Nevada. Or that rundown schoolhouse in Homer, Alaska," Rayne said.

Her mom went over to the stove and lifted the lid on a pot of stew that smelled heavenly.

"Please tell me you didn't put one of your chickens in there," Rayne said.

"Our chickens are egg producers," her father said. "We don't have any meat breeds."

Rayne stared at her dad. She had never heard him speak farmer.

"Your father spends a lot of time at the feed store," her mother explained. "But at least it keeps him out of the bars."

Rayne laughed. Her father had never been much of a drinker.

She helped her mom ladle the stew—a savory mix of vegetables and herbs—into bowls and got the butter out of the fridge while her mother cut thick slices of homemade bread and put them on a plate.

Rayne grabbed a bottle of red wine she'd brought as a gift, and the three of them sat down to eat and drink and talk about old times. Hours later, after her mother had washed the dishes and Rayne had dried them, Rayne grabbed her pajamas and makeup bag and headed for the bathroom, where her mom had a washcloth and towel set aside for her.

"Just let me know if you need anything else, sweetie," her mom said from the doorway. "It's so nice to have you here. I'm really glad you came to see us."

"Thanks for letting me show up on such short notice," Rayne said, squeezing toothpaste onto her brush.

"You're always welcome," her mom said. "Is everything OK in D.C.?"

"You mean beyond the partisan bickering in Congress and the dysfunctional local government?" She started brushing her teeth to get out of having to give an honest answer.

"Very funny," her mom said. "But you know you can talk to me if you need to, right?"

Rayne nodded, her mouth full of minty foam.

"All right, I'll leave you alone. Have a good sleep, and we'll see you in the morning."

Rayne waved, and her mom went off to bed. She rinsed and spit then she washed her face, put on her pajamas, and padded back through the kitchen to her bedroom, which was barely big enough for a twin bed, a night stand, and a little dresser. But the uncurtained window had a view beyond the barn to the moonlight shining on the woods. She took out her phone to charge it and sent Savannah a good-night text.

Then she took another look at the message from Chase. *Flying home today. I've been thinking about you. Can I stop by and see you tomorrow?*

She stared at it for a long time. Her heart was softening, and she was glad she was hundreds of miles away because otherwise she'd probably do something stupid like talk to him. And then kiss him. And then make wild love to him. And then get her heart broken all over again when he unceremoniously dumped her in favor of an assignment in East Swaziland.

She finally put the phone down and crawled under the quilt. She lay curled up on her side so she could watch the view outside. The chickens were snug in their coop, she could smell the rustic scent of wood smoke from the stove, and she felt safe and content for the first time in weeks. She'd picked the perfect hideaway.

Chapter 21

After his flight from Kathmandu, Chase made his way through Dulles airport hunched under the weight of his luggage, weary to the bone from traveling all day and crossing time zones. He felt a little feverish, which concerned him, but he was hoping a good night's sleep would fix that. And then he'd go see Rayne tomorrow and tell her he'd made a mistake and Brian Walrus was no good for her and Chase wanted her back. He thought about bringing cream puffs, or at least the filling, but he didn't want to spook her.

The thought of her naked, though, sent a little thrill through his body, which he took as a sign that his health was definitely improving.

When he got to the apartment, Colin wasn't home and Chase assumed he was at work. He dumped his bags, stripped down to his underwear, and crawled into bed. He left the door to his room ajar so he'd hear Colin when he came home.

Hours later, Chase opened his eyes to see a dark figure standing by his bed. He scrambled upright, his heart hammering.

"Jesus, you scared the shit out of me!" he said as Colin flicked on the bedside lamp.

"Didn't you hear me come in? And call your name like five times?" Colin said. Then he got a good look at Chase. "You look like shit."

"Thanks, bro. Good to see you, too." His heart was still beating hard, and he ran a hand through his matted hair.

"You should go to the doctor tomorrow."

Chase waved his hand. "Nah, I'm much better."

"If this is better, I can only imagine how bad you must have been. I'm sorry I wasn't there."

Chase felt a wave of brotherly love. "I appreciate that, man. I wish you'd been there, too. But the family that runs the guest house took good care of me."

"You're lucky they were looking out for you."

"Yeah, I know."

"Feel like drinking some beer and watching TV?" Colin asked.

"I'd love to, but I think I need to sleep. I've got some things I want to do tomorrow."

"Sure thing." Colin headed for the door and turned to say, "I'm glad you're back."

Chase slept through the night and the next morning and didn't wake up until the middle of the afternoon.

"Shit!" he said when he rolled over and looked at his alarm clock. He checked his phone, but Rayne hadn't texted back. He had a message from Colin, though, asking him to come to Zipped that night for dinner.

What day is it? Chase texted back, thinking if it was Thursday, there was a good chance Rayne might stop by.

You're seriously freaking me out, bro, Colin texted back. *It's Thursday.*

I'll be there! Chase responded.

He had plenty of time to shower, shave, unpack, and figure out what he was going to say to Rayne. He felt light-hearted and hopeful. It was good to finally be doing something positive.

Chase walked into Zipped around 7:00. The place was nearly full for trivia night and the game was already underway. As soon as Diana saw him, she set down a tray of food and came over to give him a hug. He hugged her back.

"I was worried about you," she said, giving him a playful punch in the arm. "And I don't like worrying about you. Don't ever do it again."

"Yes, ma'am!" Chase said.

Colin came around from behind the bar and gave him a quick man hug. "Good to see you up and around. You're looking a lot better than you did last night."

"Thanks. I'm feeling better, too," Chase said.

As he went back behind the bar, Colin said, "I have to admit my superpower is failing me tonight. Are you up for a beer or do you want something non-alcoholic?"

"I would love a beer," Chase said, sitting down on a stool where he could keep an eye on the door. If Rayne was already here, she'd be at the bar, so she must still be on her way. Unless....

Chase swiveled around to scan the tables but saw no sign of her. Besides, she wouldn't bring a guy like Brian Walrus to a place like Zipped.

Colin set a glass down in front of Chase, who immediately took a sip. "Best beer ever," he said.

Diana came over. "Burger, wings, fried chicken?"

Chase smiled at her. "Surprise me."

He sipped his beer and watched the door open and close and people come and go but no Rayne. The place was packed, and he was getting jostled by people squeezing next to him to get Colin's attention and order drinks. The noise and all that energy were wearing him out.

Diana brought him a plate of lightly breaded chicken with broccoli on the side, and he ate as much as he could but didn't come close to finishing it.

He flagged Colin down and leaned over the bar to ask: "Is Savannah coming tonight?"

Colin shook his head.

"What about Rayne?" Chase asked.

Colin paused before answering, as if debating what to say. Finally he said, "She's gone, bro."

"Gone?" Chase's heart hammered so hard that he could barely breathe. "What the hell does that mean? Gone where? Why?" A wave of nausea washed over him, but this time he knew it wasn't the malaria.

Colin was mixing drinks and trying to keep up with a constant stream of customers so it took him a maddeningly long time to answer. "She went to see her parents."

Chase remembered her saying her parents were hippies of

some sort, but where did they live? Think, Chase, think. Takoma Park, Maryland? For all he knew, it could be a kibbutz in Israel.

"Where do they live?" he asked.

Colin put his hand behind his ear to signal that he couldn't hear what Chase was saying.

"Where do Rayne's parents live?" he asked again, nearly shouting and feeling the strain.

"Vermont," Colin said.

"When is she coming back?"

"I don't know," Colin said. "Look, can we talk about this later. I'm kind of busy."

Diana came by to collect Chase's plate. "Still not feeling so hot, huh?" she said when she saw how little he'd eaten.

He shook his head and looked down at his watch. It was nearly 9:00 and probably too late to go to Rayne's house and ask Savannah where she was. And Chase was beat anyway. All he wanted to do was crawl into bed.

"I'm going to head home," he said. "Tell Colin I'll see him later."

"Sure thing," Diana said and gave him a sympathetic look.

He smiled. "I missed you."

"Don't get all sappy on me," she said, but she was grinning back at him. "You do not want to see me cry."

Chase woke up before noon the next day—another sign of improvement. He watched some TV, did some laundry, called his mother to let her know he was home and doing fine, but Colin had beat him to it, and mostly killed time until the workday ended.

He decided to walk over to Rayne's house. It was a cool autumn day, and leaves littered the sidewalk. The sky was turning a deep blue as the sun went down. When he rounded the corner onto Rayne's block, he noticed an elderly woman sitting on her porch. He waved, and she smiled and waved back. The friendly neighborhood suited Rayne, he thought.

He walked up onto the porch, and his heart gave a little lurch. Damn, he was nervous. But maybe nervous was good in a situation like this. Maybe it would make him seem as sincere as he was. Just as he knocked, Savannah came up the walk behind him in a pinstripe suit with a big bag over her shoulder.

She stopped when she saw him. "Hi, Chase," she said coolly. "What can I do for you?"

"Hey, Savannah. I wanted to see Rayne, but Colin told me she's out of town."

Savannah resumed walking and met him on the porch, keys in hand.

"She's gone to see her parents," she said.

"In Vermont, right?" he said, smiling and trying to look as earnest as he could. He was getting the distinct impression that Savannah had no interest in helping him.

"Yes," Savannah said as she put the key in the lock.

"Could you narrow that down for me?" he asked.

She looked up at him. "What difference does it make? Are you going to fly up there and sweep her off her feet so you can break her heart all over again?"

He took a step back, feeling as though he'd been punched in the chest. His vision swirled, and he put a hand on the wall to steady himself. He thought he saw a look of alarm or maybe pity flash across Savannah's face.

"How are you feeling?" she asked, peering at him more closely.

Chase swallowed hard, hoping that maybe Savannah's pity for his pathetic ass would translate into helping him. "I'm hanging in there," he said. "Listen, if you could—"

"Chase, I'm sorry you got sick and missed out on your assignment and everything," she said, all trace of pity gone now. "But Rayne went up there to get away from men so I don't think she'd appreciate me telling you where she is."

"Men?" Not him, but men plural. He tried to latch onto the notion that she was also fleeing Brian Walrus, but his heart was caught on the plural.

Savannah jumped back as the door flew open from the inside. A red-haired woman stood there in sweat pants and a T-shirt. "What's going on?" she asked. "I heard a knock and then keys and..." She looked at Chase then back to Savannah. "Everything OK here?"

"Yeah, Chase was just leaving."

She pushed past the woman and into the house before he could say another word.

The woman looked him up and down. "You're Chase?" she said. "Funny, I expected something different."

He knew women could be protective of one another, but he was getting irritated by the gauntlet he had to run. "I've been sick," he said. "Malaria."

She seemed to soften a bit. "That's serious," she said and started to close the door. "I hope you feel better."

"Wait! Do you know when Rayne is coming back?"

She sighed. "Just once, I'd like a guy to knock on the door looking for me. She said something about working remotely. I'd guess at least another week."

Another week? Chase couldn't wait that long. She could ignore his text messages, but maybe if he tracked down her parents' number, he could get her on the phone.

"Vermont, right? Do you know what town?"

After a moment's thought, she said, "Putney. I think it's near Brattleboro."

Chase gave her a kiss on the cheek. "You're the best! And keep answering that door—your Prince Charming will be knocking any day now."

She looked surprised, but then she smiled. "Good luck with Rayne," she said. "You're gonna need it."

Chase went straight home and googled Putney, Vermont, and anyone with the last name Michael but got nothing. He called 411, but they had no listing. It was possible that her parents didn't have a landline or didn't live right in Putney, so he looked at a map and tried some other towns nearby. Nothing.

He ate a bowl of cereal for dinner as he pondered what to do. Then he called his mother.

"Hey, Mom," he said. "Would you mind if I borrowed one of your cars?"

"Of course not," she said. "I rarely use the Sentra so you're welcome to take it for the day. Do you have errands to run? I could help if you'd like."

"Actually, I was thinking of taking a road trip to Vermont."

There was a puzzled silence at the other end of the line. "Why Vermont?" she finally said. "Don't you think you should be taking it easy for a while?"

He hadn't even given any thought to making up a story. And this was his mom anyway. She had a way of seeing right through him.

"There's this girl... uh, woman...."

"The same *woman* you worked on the gala with?" she asked, her voice brightening. "Rayne, right?"

"I screwed up, Mom, and she's gone off to Vermont and I really need to talk to her."

"Have you tried calling her? How do you know she'll even be there when you get there? You might drive right past each other on the highway."

"I'm out of options, so I'll have to take that chance. She's supposed to be staying another week. And she's not responding to my messages."

"Chase, honey, maybe you should just let this one go. If she's not—"

"No! I mean, I tried, but I just can't," he said. "We had a misunderstanding and now she thinks I'm a heartless womanizer and maybe I was but I'm not anymore. And I drove her right into the arms of Brian Walrus, and all I know is that I have to try to fix it."

"Sweetie, you're not making any sense."

He ran his hand through his hair, eyes bleary, heart hammering. "Can I please just borrow the car for a few days?"

"I'll make you a deal. You can have the car, but only if you come to the house tonight and stay over. I want to make sure you're fit to go off on a trip alone."

He couldn't help but laugh. "Mom, I've gone on dozens of trips to way more dangerous places than Vermont on my own."

"Don't remind me. But you've been very sick, and I don't

think you're thinking straight. I'll send a car to pick you up in an hour. Will you have your things packed by then?"

"I'll be packed in five minutes," he said, smiling. "And thanks, Mom. For the car and the concern."

"You're my son," she said simply. "And I love you."

When Chase got to the house, his mother had fixed a turkey sandwich for him with cole slaw and potato chips on the side. She sat with him in the kitchen while he ate, his appetite slowly coming back.

"I met Rayne at the gala," she said. "Beautiful girl. And very sweet."

"That's her," he said. "Did you and Dad buy any art that night?"

"Your father didn't go. He had to work at the last minute. I was going to stay home, but Jeremy Banks had sent me those lovely flowers and it seemed rude not to go."

Chase grinned. "Jeremy is quite the draw."

She gave him a playful swat. "I'm a happily married woman."

He almost said, "Really?" but stopped himself in time.

"Colin says the event was a big success," Chase said.

"Yes, all that hard work you and Rayne did really paid off, and she did a lovely job setting everything up. The house was just beautiful. They exceeded their fundraising goal, and some man named Brandon Wallace bought all your photographs."

"He did, huh?" The thought gave Chase a creepy feeling, and he wondered if he had the option of refusing to sell to him.

"Maybe you should send him a note," his mother said.

"Yeah, maybe I should," Chase said. But if he did, it wouldn't be about photography.

His mother made him go to bed as soon as he was done eating, and Chase couldn't deny there was something soothing about sleeping in his childhood room. He shook his head at himself and chalked it up to the lingering effects of malaria.

The next morning when he came downstairs, his mom was waiting in the kitchen. She handed him the keys to the car and

...

said, "I'm not thrilled about this, but since you seem to be so determined to go, I won't stop you."

He kissed her on the cheek. "I'll call you from the road, OK?"

"Please do," she said, handing him a thermos of hot tea and a sandwich.

"Gee, where's my Spider-Man lunch box?"

She smiled. "You're a grown-up now, remember?"

Chase drove out of the city and into Maryland. It was a sunny Saturday morning, and traffic was light. He had a GPS app running on his phone, which sat in the cup holder between the seats, and he listened to NPR on the radio until he got out of range of the city. Then he turned it off. He didn't need the distraction because his mind was whirring. He had no idea how Rayne would react to him just showing up. But he hoped the effort would be enough to convince her to listen to what he had to say.

He stopped around lunchtime at a rest area and ate his sandwich outside at a picnic table and called his mom to say he was doing fine. But he didn't linger because it was cold and a little windy, and he didn't like sitting still. He wanted to keep moving.

He drove through Brattleboro at dinner time and kept heading north. He saw the signs for Putney and followed Route 5 into town—which was small, and everything seemed to have already closed up for the night. He was starting to panic when he saw a feed store that was still open.

He parked and dashed inside. The place smelled of hay and sawdust. He was expecting the counter to be manned by a guy in a flannel shirt and a John Deere cap, but the middle-aged man at the cash register had a gold earring and long gray hair pulled back in a pony tail.

"Can I help you?" the man asked.

"I hope so," Chase said. "I'm looking for the Michaels. I understand they live around here."

"Judy and Wesley?" the guy said.

"I guess so. I'm actually a friend of their daughter's."

The guy's face brightened. "You're a friend of Rayne's?"

It didn't surprise Chase that Rayne had already wormed her way into the community. "Yeah, but I forgot the address. Could you tell me how to get there, by any chance?"

Chase pulled out his phone, prepared to type directions into his notepad app.

"Their place is just up the hill. Go out here and make your first left, then go right when you come to a T-intersection and just follow your nose. Their farm is right before you run out of road. Can't miss it."

Chase paused with his thumbs poised to type. How the hell was he going to follow those directions? No street names, no traffic signals. He put his phone away and thanked the guy. He'd just have to go as far as he could and ask someone when he got close.

Chapter 22

For the past couple of days, Rayne had helped with the chores in the morning—feeding the chickens and bringing in firewood—and then her mom went to her job teaching English at the Putney School while her dad stayed home. He had a little side business repairing small engines, and she spent her first afternoon watching him fix the neighbor's snow blower while they talked about nothing in particular.

The next day, she went with him to buy chicken feed and straw at the store in town then helped him replace some rotten boards in the barn wall as he told her what he knew about raising sheep and the best dog breeds for protecting them from coyotes and wolves. She had always loved helping her dad when she was a kid. Maybe he would have really liked a son, but she never felt like he treated her differently because she was a girl.

On Saturday morning, she and her mom visited the spinnery in town to see about having their future sheep's wool spun into yarn. It was run by a cooperative, which pleased her mother, and the floor was dusted with bits of fluff and smelled like wet wool. Rayne browsed through the yarn for sale in the shop. It had a wonderfully nubby texture, and she wondered if she should take up knitting.

Saturday evening, they were feeding the chickens when her mother asked, "Do you feel like talking about it yet?"

"Talking about what?" Rayne said, though she knew what her mom meant.

"The guy who made you run away up here."

"Not a guy," she said, putting the chicken feed in the tray. Now she could maneuver confidently around the birds, aware of how they moved and no longer afraid of stepping on them. "There were two of them."

Her mom raised an eyebrow. "That doesn't sound like you."

"I wasn't dating them at the same time, Mom!"

"OK, so which one made you run away?"

Rayne sighed. "The first one." Then she realized that, technically, Brandon came before Chase. "He's the brother of the guy Savannah's been seeing. He's a professional photographer with a serious case of wanderlust and commitment phobia. He has a habit of booking gigs in remote corners of the world when he needs to get out a relationship. Everyone warned me about him, but I fell for him anyway."

"I see. And where did *he* run off to?"

The way her mom emphasized the word "he" made Rayne look at her. "Nepal. And he was running away because things were starting to get good. Serious maybe. And he didn't want that."

"Maybe he was scared. Men get scared, too, you know."

"Why are you defending him, Mom? You've never even met him."

Her mother walked outside and Rayne followed. The sun was going down and the temperature was dropping, but she was getting used to the crisp, clean air.

"You said people warned you about him," her mother said. "Maybe you let everyone else decide for you. Maybe you didn't give him a chance to do the right thing."

The thought made Rayne uncomfortable, and she put the scoop back in the barrel of cracked corn and fastened the lid in silence.

"Have you heard from him at all since he left?" her mother asked.

Rayne shrugged. "He sent a few texts, but I've been ignoring him." In response to the look her mother gave her, she added, "He was working with me on the gala, and then he took this assignment and wasn't even there for the event. It hurt, you know? And how could I ever compete with the allure of Nepal or Timbuktu or anyplace else?"

Her mom latched the coop door shut. "You could go with him."

Rayne looked at her, trying to process the notion.

"I know your childhood wasn't ideal and you would have liked to stay in one place longer," her mother said. "Someplace 'normal.' But you always managed to make friends and create a community. Remember how you organized the kids in Trumansburg, New York, to clean up that stretch of the lake shore?"

Rayne laughed. "Yeah. I think some of them were the kids who put the trash there in the first place." She smiled to think of it now. That's where she'd met Carol, who was all knobby knees and freckles back then, and they'd stayed friends all these years.

She turned to her mom. "I know I've been hard on you and Dad, but lately I've been thinking my childhood wasn't so terrible. It was actually kind of wonderful in a lot of ways. I'm not saying I'm going to run off and join a commune, but all that traveling we did—I forgot how a change of scenery can give you a whole new perspective. I was lucky to have that."

Her mom gave her a big hug. "I'm so glad to hear you say that. I've been worried. You never seem to want to visit us, and I was afraid you hated us. That's also how I knew something was up when you asked to visit on such short notice."

"You know me too well," Rayne said with a laugh.

Her mom tucked a strand of hair behind Rayne's ear. "And the other guy? You said there were two."

"I don't want to ruin your opinion of me. Let's just say he was an old flame who came back around, and I lost my head."

"OK, we can leave it at that," her mom said. Then she put her arm through Rayne's, and they headed up to the house.

Surprisingly enough, Chase managed to follow the guy's directions. He had to go slow because his mom's Sentra wasn't made for rutted dirt roads, but fifteen minutes later, he pulled into a driveway behind a battered pickup truck.

He turned off the engine, and his heart was pounding. Then he saw her and was sure his heart would give out.

She was walking up from the hill in the fading sunlight with her arm around an older woman who must be her mom. They were laughing and bumping hips together. Rayne was wearing black leggings and boots and a long cable knit sweater with a colorful silk scarf wound around her neck. Her cheeks were rosy from the cold, and her hair was tousled in that way he found so appealing. He took a moment to watch her, drinking in the sight of her felt like a tonic.

Finally, he got out of the car and stood beside it with his hand on top of the open door, suddenly shy and unsure of what to do next. Her mother noticed him first, then Rayne looked up and saw him.

She stopped, stunned to see Chase standing in the driveway. For a split second, she wondered if he was a hallucination. But she didn't think her heart would have taken flight the way it did if he was.

"Why are you…How did…How did you find me?" she sputtered.

Her mother slipped away to the house and went inside. Rayne stayed where she was, and Chase found that he was frozen to the spot, too.

"Your roommate told me you were in Putney."

Her roommate. Rayne wondered why he would refer to Savannah that way, and then realized he must mean Carol.

"I stopped at the feed store in town," Chase said, "and the guy told me where your parents live."

She stared at him, still trying to come to grips with his sudden appearance. "It's a long drive," she said.

"Yeah, I know. But I needed to talk to you." He looked awkward, which wasn't like him, and seemed to be struggling to find the words. "I needed to tell you I'm sorry."

It was a start. "OK," she said slowly, telling herself not to get swept away on this one grand gesture. "What are you sorry for?"

He stepped around the car door. "For missing the gala and going off to Nepal instead."

She studied him for a moment. He certainly sounded sincere, and she didn't think he'd drive nine hours to lie to her. "OK. Apology accepted." She was trying to keep her voice neutral, but her stomach was doing somersaults as she wondered what else he'd come to tell her.

He took another step toward her, looking pale and thin, and her heart ached to think of how sick he must have been.

"And for not telling you how I feel."

"About what?" Rayne asked, her heart starting to pound.

He stepped close enough to reach out and touch her, but he didn't.

"About you," he said.

"What about me?" Her voice caught in her throat. It was taking everything she had not to throw her arms around him. But she had to hear him out, she had to be sure this time.

"That I want to be with you, all in, one hundred percent. If you give me another chance, Rayne, I swear I'll never leave you like that again. I can't breathe without you."

"You seem to be doing all right," she teased even as tears started to cloud her vision.

"Because you're here," he said, his voice rough. "Please tell me I'm not too late. Please tell me I can fix this."

Before he could finish, Rayne had launched herself at him, and he wrapped his arms around her, holding her tight against him as he buried his face in her neck and, for the first time since getting off the plane, finally felt like he was home.

"When I was delirious, I hallucinated about you and Brian Walrus," he said, his lips grazing her hair. "And then Colin told me that you'd gone to dinner with him, and I was afraid that I'd lost you, lost the best thing that ever happened to me."

Rayne pulled back so she could look him in the face. "Brian Walrus?" When she saw that he was serious, she smiled. "You really are terrible with names."

Chase kept staring at her, and she realized he was waiting for an answer.

"You didn't lose me," she said, her voice low and full of emotion. "I never stopped thinking about you."

Chase broke into a smile that lit up his eyes and warmed Rayne's heart. He brushed her hair away from her face. "That's good news, sweetheart," he said in his Humphrey Bogart voice, which made her laugh. "Because I am hopelessly, head-over-heels in love with you."

By the end of the sentence, he was back to his own voice, and Rayne's expression turned serious. A feeling of panic flashed through him, but he was glad he'd said it. It felt good to be honest.

She cupped his face in her hands and said in her best forties film star voice, "I never loved him. It was you—it was always you. Dammit, kid, I can't live without you."

Then she drew him closer and kissed him, and he plunged his hands in her hair and kissed her back like he never meant to stop. Which would have been fine with her.

When they finally paused to catch their breath, he pressed his forehead against hers and clasped his hands at the small of her back. "I'm totally serious, you know," he said. "About loving you."

"I know," she said softly, reaching up to touch his cheek. "I love you, too."

He sighed deeply and closed his eyes.

"Have you ever been to Nova Scotia?" she asked.

He pulled her close and planted a firm kiss on the top of her head before saying, "No, I never have."

"Me either. Want to take a road trip?"

He gripped her tighter, and she felt snug and warm against his chest.

"I'd follow you anywhere," he said.

Check out the Capitol Love Series Book 3:

The Sweet Spot...

Crystal McAlister's bakery, Sweet Happens, consumes almost every minute of her life. Except for the time she devotes to the wrong kinds of men. Men who are all talk and no action—unless they're all action and no talk. So she's decided to swear off men and funnel her energy into expanding her business. A local restaurant mogul is willing to be an investor, but only if Crystal moves into the digital age. Considering that she can barely work her iPhone, this could be a deal breaker for her dream. Except that she's just met an adorable technology whiz.

When his father died, Kyle Richardson was left with a small inheritance and the realization that he's only ever done what was expected of him. On a whim, he uprooted himself and moved cross-country to Washington, D.C., for a job as an IT director at a small nonprofit. When he isn't working or taking long runs along the Potomac River, he's tinkering with computers. But figuring out who he wants to be is proving harder than he thought, and he's feeling a little lost—until he crosses paths with Crystal, who is more enchanting and lively than any woman he's ever known.

Kyle could hold the key to Crystal's future, but can she convince him to come out of his shell long enough to help her? And can she do it without violating her ban on falling in love?

About the Author

Samantha Powers lived in the Washington, D.C., area for several years and worked in various corporate and nonprofit jobs while writing in her spare time. She now lives in Vermont, where she can indulge her passion for walks in the woods, writing full time, and maple-flavored everything. She also loves animals, reality TV, and cupcakes.

The first book in the Capitol Love series, *The Plan*, was published in December 2015 and is available on Amazon.com. Her short story "Portrait of a Lover" appears in the *Trick or Treat!* anthology published in October 2015.

Follow her on Twitter: @CapitolLover or
Facebook: CapitolLoveSeries